KILLMASTER IN DISGUISE

"Step aside," came the raspy voice from the center of the room. "And shut the door."

The woman stepped aside, pushing the door closed as she moved.

Carlos Panama stood in the center of the room, a silenced Walther in his hand, its deadly muzzle moving idly back and forth to cover both Lapita and Carter.

"You . . . raise your hands!"

Carter raised his left arm, high.

"Both of them!"

"I cannot, *senhor*. My right arm is crippled."

Suddenly Panama was laughing, long and loud.

"Dear God, you whore, you mean this is your lover? Who are you?"

"I am the man, *senhor,*" Carter replied, "who has come to kill you."

NICK CARTER IS IT!

FROM THE NICK CARTER KILLMASTER SERIES

NICK CARTER

KILLMASTER

ASSIGNMENT: RIO

CHARTER BOOKS, NEW YORK

ASSIGNMENT: RIO

A Charter Book/published by arrangement with
The Condé Nast Publications, Inc.

PRINTING HISTORY
Charter Original/August 1984

ISBN: 0-441-03223-0

Charter Books are published by The Berkley Publishing Group,
200 Madison Avenue, New York, N.Y. 10016
PRINTED IN THE UNITED STATES OF AMERICA

Dedicated to the men of the
Secret Services of the United
States of America

ONE

RIO: NOW

His eyes snapped open. No movement other than the pupils as they rolled around the hotel room. There was no groggy remnant of sleep. He was instantly alert and awake.

An arm came up, and red numbers flashed from the black face on his wrist: 5:59:55. As usual, the unerring alarm in his brain had been five seconds faster than the mechanical one on his wrist. He touched the tiny button that would stop the buzz and slid like an uncoiling panther from the bed.

With the same grace, his nude body moved to the window, every muscle rippling in the tall, lean frame like riffs being played on the keys of a player piano.

Nine stories below lay Brazil's bistro-by-the-sea, Rio. In the distance, Santos Dumont Airport and Sugar Loaf Mountain jutted out to embrace Guanabara Bay like an anxious woman's arms embracing an azure lover.

Directly below, near-naked tanned bodies and others with gaudy tourist apparel were already filling the mosaic sidewalks leading down to the beach and bay.

The city had begun to blossom with the bunting of carnival. It was still two weeks away, but preparations had been going on for a month, practically since the day of his arrival.

For the first time since moving from the bed, the dark, smooth-featured face changed expression. The almost vacant, always moving eyes held, fixed on the center of the bay, and the lips curved into a smile.

One month of laborious preparation in Paris, London, and Miami, and four weeks in Rio itself, would end in just ten hours. The most intricate operation of his long and diversified career would be over and, he was positive, successful.

A violent shudder, almost sexual, passed through his body. All thoughts died except of the present mission. It was as it had to be. He turned and moved with purpose into the tiny bath.

Quickly, with deft, experienced fingers, the face lightened in color, gray replaced the raven sheen of his hair, and wrinkles of age appeared on his throat and hands.

Back at the bed, he moved into a dark blue suit of expensive material and the perfect cut of a London tailor. Over this went a light gray suit of a much cheaper fabric. It was heavily padded, stained, and rumpled.

This accomplished, he pulled open the closet door and stood in front of the mirror on its inner side. He took a deep, deep breath and then slowly expelled it. The neck shortened as the shoulders sagged. Inches came off his height and were added to his girth as the body seemed to evaporate and then swell inside the suit.

Again he smiled. But this time it was nearly a leer, a

cynical old man looking out at the world through tired eyes.

Carefully he removed his fingerprints from every part of the room. The remaining clothing was checked for stray hairs and to make sure he hadn't missed a label. When he came across the uniform of a lieutenant in the army of President Frederico Tejada, he allowed himself a light chuckle. He wadded it into a ball and jammed it into a decaying piece of plasterboard in the back of the closet.

Let them find that last, he thought, *if they find it at all*. It should pose some interesting questions.

Questions that he knew would never be answered.

He stored the makeup and other toilet articles in the dumpy suit.

From under the pillow he produced a 9mm Luger in an ankle-wrap holster. The clip checked full. Two snaps and it was firmly attached just under the calf of his right leg. On his left leg, in the same place, nestled in a chamois sheath, was a pencil-thin stiletto.

Thin briefcase in hand, he did a last check of the room, nodded, and went out the door.

Two minutes later he passed through the lobby. He didn't bother checking out or paying the bill. He wouldn't be back anyway, and no one would suspect that the slumped, shuffling old man going out was the tall, dapper Englishman who had checked in.

And no one would ever know that neither man ever existed, that beneath both suits of clothes and identities was the deadliest agent the U.S. could send into the field.

Nick Carter, Killmaster.

TWO

WASHINGTON, D.C.:
EIGHT WEEKS BEFORE

It was just past midnight. One lone window gleamed on the very top floor of the Amalgamated Press and Wire Services Building on Dupont Circle.

The bottom two floors were given over to the legitimate news-gathering arm. The upper six floors were operations and control centers for the U.S. government's ultrasecret arm, AXE.

Behind the half-shaded window, the chief of AXE, David Hawk, sat in a cloud of cigar smoke. To his right sat sable-haired Ginger Bateman, his secretary-cum-first assistant.

Both the man's and the woman's eyes were riveted on their top operative: Nick Carter, N3.

Carter himself was going over last-minute plans, both in his mind and with the papers before him.

"What do you think?" Hawk rasped.

"I think everything has been covered, but it's still one hell of a gamble."

"I didn't say it wasn't when I first proposed it."

"It means impersonating five, maybe six people and fooling at least fifteen with the disguises."

"At least," Ginger Bateman said, shaking her lustrous hair back and leaning closer to Carter. "No one must know your true identity, first of all . . . and, most of all, must never suspect that you are in any way connected with the United States government."

"I can see why," Carter said, rubbing fingertips over his temples. "AXE involvement in the internal politics of other nations has been pretty taboo in the past."

"It still is, perhaps more than ever," Hawk said. "But this is a special case . . . a *very* special case. If Frederico Tejada remains the president of Brazil, the country will go further to hell."

Carter nodded. "And if General Pablo Fernandes becomes president, he will send the country deeper into bankruptcy . . . and, eventually, rebellion."

"And if there is open rebellion," Ginger added, "it might well result in a Marxist Brazil."

"So," Carter sighed, "I become kingmaker and make sure that a third party—someone completely neutral and a true Brazilian patriot—takes over the reins of government."

"That's it in a nutshell," Hawk said. "And because of the touchiness of the situation, it must be a one-man job. You'll do your own setups and wash them away when the job is completed. It must not be questioned in any way that the man we want in power assumes that power because of a series of coincidences, freak accidents, and his own ability."

"And the CIA is involved," Carter said.

"Yes, but they know nothing of you or what's coming down. They'll be on the scene for other reasons. Eventually, even their files will record the fact that our man came to power without our help."

Carter smiled, reached forward, and dropped the sheaf of papers on Hawk's desk.

"And what if our man becomes *their* man once he gets in power?"

Hawk returned the smile. "The indications are that he won't. In any event, that's State's job. Ours is to put him there."

"Did you get everything from Willie Geis in New York?" Ginger asked.

Carter nodded.

Willie Geis was a genius who ran an exclusive hair salon in the Big Apple. Most of his customers were the blond- and blue-haired matrons from Westchester and other suburbs who could wile away two-hundred-dollar afternoons under his practiced hands and hair dryers.

Actually, the salon was a legitimate front for Willie. Half of his work—the more expensive half—was done for AXE.

Willie's genius was in makeup and disguise.

Carter had spent two full days with Willie in the past week.

The result was five completely different characters, right down to their passports.

Hawk stood and moved around the desk. In a rare gesture, he placed his hand on Carter's shoulder and squeezed.

"It'll be rough, Nick. You'll have to totally submerge. Worse yet, both Tejada and Fernandes know we don't

want them in power. They suspect we might send someone in. That's why the CIA smoke screen. If they even
suspect that you're bulling them . . ."

Hawk's voice trailed off. Carter smiled and rolled his
eyes up to meet those of his superior.

"If they suspect, I can't waste them and run."

"No way. Not unless there's no smell of our involvement. Okay?"

"I guess it will have to be," Carter replied.

"Good." Hawk moved back to his chair, the tension in
his body obviously dispelled. "Now, about tonight.
You've seduced the woman?"

Carter glanced at Ginger Bateman. Her eyes were lowered. They had had a holiday fling once. It was good, very
good. Ever since, Carter had tried to rekindle it.

It had been no dice.

"Maybe," she had told him. "Someday, when we're
both out of this racket."

"By then we'll probably be too old," Carter had replied. "And, besides, I don't think I can ever quit."

"Why, Nick? Good God, *why*?"

It was hard to explain. It was something, a philosophy
at the core of his gut. Most men wait for the second before
death to experience all of life. They do this, and waste
their lives in a dream.

Not Nick Carter.

He needed to live on the edge, to experience every
moment of his life as if it were the moment before death.

But Ginger wouldn't have understood.

So he didn't tell her.

He had just shrugged.

"More like she has verbally seduced me," Carter said
to Hawk. "The real seduction is tonight. I'm to pick her

up two blocks from the embassy at two sharp.''

"And she still believes that you're convinced of her defection?''

"Absolutely.''

Hawk checked his watch. "How long will it take you to drive up to the cabin?''

"About an hour . . . not much more.''

"Then I'll hear by five A.M.?''

"Definitely. I'll take the late flight to London out of Boston tomorrow night.''

"Nasty business,'' Hawk growled, chewing his cigar harder than usual. "But then, it becomes easier when you know that they mean to kill you.''

"A lot easier,'' Carter replied.

"Good luck, N3.''

Carter nodded at Hawk and crossed the room. At the door he threw a glance at Ginger Bateman.

Her eyes wouldn't leave her lap.

Carter parked the Mustang in the near darkness between two streetlights, lit a cigarette, and slumped back in the seat to wait.

The shuttle had been right on time from Washington. Finding the company Mustang and driving in from La Guardia had taken exactly forty minutes at this hour of the morning.

It was now five minutes until two.

Idly, he went through what he hoped would be the events of the next few hours.

They would drive to the cabin and become very intimate. Eventually they would make love. Sometime afterward—while Carter was sated with wine and sex— Vassily Petrovitch would slug Carter and kill him.

Carter wondered if they would let it look like an assassination or if they would go to the trouble of making it look like an accident.

Probably the latter. Much less messy on American soil.

In any event, that wouldn't be the way it happened.

A figure rounded the corner a block behind the car, bringing Carter upright in the seat.

She was wearing a white blouse, a short leather jacket, and a mid-calf-length skirt that was slit up one side nearly to her hip.

The slit opened wide with each step she took toward the Mustang.

Lila Palenkov had very nice legs.

Lila Palenkov, born thirty-one years before in Moscow. She was trained by the KGB originally as a cipher clerk. Because of her striking beauty and ample physical endowments, she was soon transferred to foreign intelligence as a decoy.

What did she decoy?

Politicians, businessmen, and, most recently, agents. She got them to reveal military or industrial secrets, or led them to their deaths.

She had come to the United States six months earlier as part of the Soviet delegation to the United Nations.

Through leaks, the CIA and the FBI had heard rumors that her target was a high-level agent in a high-level agency.

AXE discovered the agent when Lila had "accidentally" run into—and tried to set up a friendship with—Nick Carter.

"Pursue it," Hawk had said. "Maybe we can use it."

The words had proved providential. The Brazil caper had become a necessity.

When Lila made her pitch at last to Carter that she wanted to defect—and AXE learned that Vassily Petrovitch had slipped into the country through Canada—it all fell into place.

Carter played along until the Brazil mission was set before he agreed to help Lila defect.

In a way, Carter thought, this was balm for his ego.

The Soviets thought him a big enough thorn in their sides to kill him and had sent Petrovitch—their top assassin—to do the job.

She was two feet from the passenger door when Carter leaned across the seat and threw it open. She slipped into the seat and exposed a generous amount of well-rounded, panty-hose-clad thigh as she slid across into his arms.

"Nick, oh Nick . . ."

Her lips were soft, slightly parted, and warm as they met his. The kiss was practiced, as carefully executed as the press of a firm, ample breast against his arm.

Carter traded hot, darting tongues with her for several seconds, then slowly disengaged his arms.

"Were you followed?"

"No. I'm sure of it."

Carter suppressed a smile. He was sure of it too.

There would be no need to follow them tonight, the night of Lila's defection. Vassily Petrovitch had already followed Carter to the cabin two days before when Carter had set up the Russian woman's "hideaway."

Carter shoved the Mustang into gear and slid away from the curb. He moved in from the river past the U.N. building and turned uptown at Third Avenue.

"Scared?"

"Of course I am," she lied. "But I feel safe with you. Just think . . . a whole new life."

"Yeah," Carter replied, barely able to keep the dryness out of his voice that he felt in his throat.

He played games just above midtown on the East Side. He zigzagged between First and Third, went uptown for a while, only to cut back downtown for a few blocks.

When he was sure that Lila was convinced that he was just making sure they didn't have a tail, he cut over to the West Side and headed north for the Taconic State Parkway, Westchester, and beyond.

"It's going to be wonderful, Nick, darling . . . just you and me . . . a little house for a month . . . just the two of us . . ."

"Yeah, wonderful," he replied, hardly feeling the hand inching up his thigh.

"You didn't tell your superiors yet about this, did you?" she asked, her hand very high now, her sensual lips brushing his jaw line.

"Of course not, Lila. I've done everything just as you requested."

"Wonderful!," she breathed in his ear. "It will give us time together, and it will be . . . how do you say . . . ?"

"A feather in my cap when I give you over to my people and you give them all the ciphers you have in your head."

"Yes . . . yes, you will be a hero!"

Lady, Carter thought, glancing at his watch, *I already am*.

It was three o'clock in the morning.

The five-room cabin was rustic but well appointed.

Small talk, chitchat, and brief, intimate touches took up the first twenty minutes after Carter brought the bags in from the car.

He purposely made three trips when one would have

been enough. During those trips he checked the wires and cables he had previously installed on all the windows and doors as a warning and silent alarm system.

He did it carefully, surreptitiously. Somewhere out there in the woods and the darkness, Carter knew that Vassily Petrovitch was waiting.

It was risky, exposing himself time after time against the lights of the house.

But it was a calculated risk.

When he didn't draw sniper fire during the trips, Carter was fairly sure they planned on making his execution look like an accident.

When the cabin was secure and the bags were in the large master bedroom, he had descended the short flight of stairs to the living room.

Lila was waiting near the open bar, two drinks in hand.

"Here you are, darling, a drink . . . before. Scotch, ice, and a twist. You see how I remember?"

Carter accepted the glass and slid his arm around her.

"Will you miss Russia?"

"Of course I will," she replied, lifting her body to her toes, bringing her lips close to his. "But life will be better for me here in your country."

Carter kissed her, holding it as long as necessary, and then he moved his face into her hair. He brought the drink up to her shoulder and jiggled the ice as if he were sipping it.

Actually, he sniffed it.

He smelled nothing, but that didn't mean anything.

A strong sedative combined with alcohol can be rendered odorless and tasteless.

"To tomorrow," Lila said, moving away from him and raising her glass.

"To tonight," Carter countered with a smile.

Her eyes, over the rim of her glass, bored into his throat. Carter drank lustily, exaggerating each swallow to make his Adam's apple bounce.

The maneuver brought the warmest smile to her lips that Carter had ever seen there.

"Bed?" she said.

"Bed it is," he replied. "You go on up. I'll get the lights."

To throw her further, Carter killed the rest of the drink while she crossed the room, her eyes darting over her shoulder every third step.

In the kitchen, Carter withdrew a packet of a powerful antidepressant drug Hawk had given him. He quickly swallowed two tablets and washed them down with warm water.

By the time he had extinguished the lights and started up the stairs, he could sense the two powerful drugs combating each other in his body.

Even the antidepressant was having a little trouble winning. In the bedroom doorway, a sudden lightheadedness struck him. He swayed slightly and grabbed the jamb to steady himself.

"Is something wrong?"

Pure innocence, face and voice.

The rest of her was just the opposite. She was stark naked, and the room's dimmed lights danced provocatively over her creamy skin.

"It's nothing," Carter countered, still swaying slightly as he crossed the room.

He stood beside the bed, removing his own clothes and letting his eyes roam over her body.

Lila Palenkov was everything he had envisioned she

would be under the rather shapeless clothes she habitually wore. Her ample breasts were perfectly shaped, the pinkish-brown tips already jutting toward his caress. Her belly was pleasingly rounded, and her hips flowed beautifully into her tapering thighs.

As Carter edged his own naked body over the side of the bed, he could swear she actually looked downright demure.

As the wiry hair on his chest pressed against her nipples, Lila reached up and drew him to her. They kissed, and Carter molded his flesh to hers.

For a wild moment he thought he wouldn't be able to perform, and it was imperative that he did. He wanted to give Petrovitch all the time in the world to get into the house.

And then her hands began to explore his body. She did it so well, with such an expert touch, that his passion surmounted the feeling of distaste.

"I want you," he growled, putting a slur in his speech.

Her hands ceased their teasing and she lay back, her thighs spread to take him.

"Yes, Nick, I want you, too . . . so badly."

I know you do, Carter thought. *A little sexual exercise will make the Mickey you gave me work ten times as fast!*

He moved over her body and felt her hands grope and find him. It was done deftly, expertly. One second he was poised above her, and the next he was deep inside her.

She gasped and surged up against him. Her hips ground and twisted, making her female warmth close over him like a soft, damp cocoon.

Carter ignored the tinge of phoniness in her gasps and the almost too practiced gyrations of her curvacious body as he thrust deeply, almost savagely, into her.

At the same time, his eyes moved to the clock-radio beside the bed.

The alarm light glowed a bright red.

Vassily Petrovitch was in the house.

The reality of it brought a smile to Carter's lips and more adrenaline to his body.

He gave himself up to the euphoria of sex. He let it capture his brain and made it appear as if he were slowly falling into the fog of the sedative.

When his climax came, Carter let it sweep him away. He used the flood of release to relax his whole body until he slumped over her in apparent sleep.

"Nick . . . Nick . . ."

She felt the beat of his heart with one hand and raised an eyelid with the other. When she was completely satisfied, she unceremoniously rolled him away and slipped from the bed.

From a slitted eye, Carter watched her perfect buttocks jiggle across the room and disappear into the hall.

Quickly he rolled from the bed and rummaged in one of the nearby suitcases. When his hand closed over the stubby CO_2 pistol, he moved back into the bed.

"Vassily . . . Vassily, are you here?" Lila's voice came from somewhere around the stairs.

"Is it done?"

Carter guessed Petrovitch was somewhere in the kitchen. Then he heard the man's footsteps.

"Yes. Have you rigged his car?"

"It's ready. Dress him, and I'll come up and get him in a minute."

On the bed, Carter smiled. Carbon monoxide. Suicide.

It happens. Agents on the edge are like burned-out cops. The last life they take is often their own.

He heard her bare feet pad back down the hall, and he moved the snout of the CO_2 pistol even with his side, pointed upward.

He sensed rather than saw her cross the room and lean over the bed. He felt her fingers curl on the sheet over his chest.

When she pulled it away, Carter opened his eyes, adjusted his aim, and fired.

The sound was no louder than a sudden escape of air from a small vent. The needle's thin sliver of steel tipped with a deadly poison struck just left of her breastbone.

Her face registered a microsecond of shock just before the steel tip pierced her heart and the poison spread its rampant toxin.

Carter rolled away just as she fell across the bed. Instantly he was galvanized into action. He covered her lifeless body with the sheet, leaving part of a foot exposed at the side and the barest suggestion of hair on the pillow.

Slipping into his shorts and pants, he dimmed the lights just a bit more and scattered his shirt, tie, and coat over her body. Then he moved into the bathroom, snapped on the light, left the door two inches ajar, and turned on the hot water faucet full blast.

The last thing he did was to climb into the shower and pull the curtain. Then he tugged a second sliver of steel from the pistol's butt and slipped it into the firing chamber.

Minutes later, over the sound of the water, he heard Vassily Petrovitch call out from the bedroom doorway.

"Lila . . . Lila, what are you doing?"

The bathroom door slammed against the tub as Petrovitch entered.

Carter threw the curtain aside and aimed through the

steam at the Russian's blurred image.

Petrovitch was just turning toward the sound when the steel shaft slid through his temple and entered his brain.

He fell like a rock.

Carter stepped over the corpse and tugged him to the bed, where he deposited him beside Lila. Quickly, he undressed the man and redressed himself in the Russian's shirt and suit. The fit was far from perfect, but it would do for now.

Carter placed all his own ID in the pocket of his suit jacket. With the jacket over his arm and two of his bags in hand, he made his way downstairs.

He hung the jacket on a rack by the front door and placed one of the bags beneath it. The second bag he carried out to the garage.

Petrovitch had the Mustang rigged, all right. Two hoses were attached to the exhaust pipes and jammed through the passenger side window, with towels stuffed into the rest of the cracks.

Carter derigged the car, buried the hoses in the surrounding woods, and then fanned out at a jog along the three narrow lanes that fed into the main road nearby.

He found Petrovitch's wheels about two miles up the second lane, pulled up beneath some trees.

It was a late-model Chevrolet sedan, and the key in the pocket of the jacket Carter wore fitted the ignition.

Back at the house, he hauled a small, portable X-ray machine out of the Mustang's trunk and went back upstairs.

It took him about a half hour to get plates of Vassily Petrovitch's teeth. When he was sure he had a perfect set, he took plates and machine back down and stored them in the trunk of the Chevrolet, then returned to the room one last time.

This time with one of Willie Geis's makeup kits in hand.

Carefully and meticulously, with a mirror propped up on the bed between himself and the corpse's face, he made a facial transformation.

It took nearly an hour of work with facial putty, spirit gum, and false hair. But by the end of that time, only the man's wife or immediate superiors could have told the difference between N. Carter and V. Petrovitch.

Finished at last with the disguise, he built and stoked a good-size fire in the fireplace.

Satisfied, he rechecked the new feeder jets he had installed on the room's gas heaters. They weren't really new. They were worn and leaked badly. A single roll of toilet paper strewn around the room and into the fireplace would do the rest.

The last thing he did before climbing into the Chevrolet was turn the gas on at the outside tanks.

He was just turning onto the main highway that would eventually take him to Boston, when the predawn air was rocked with an ear-shattering explosion.

Through the car's rear window he saw a fireball shoot into the air over a hundred feet, and he smiled.

In less than a half hour, most of the house and the bodies would be cinders.

During the drive, Carter went through his pockets. The wallet was full of European and American bank credit cards in the same name as the passport: Henri Devonovitch.

According to the cards and passport, Devonovitch was a Canadian citizen living in Toronto.

Carter stopped for gas at Worcester, paid for it with one of Devonovitch/Petrovitch's credit cards, and was pleased when he copied the signature swirl-perfect.

If it was checked later, it would be too late anyway.

From the pumps he pulled the car around to the side of the adjoining diner and slid into a space beside a long Cadillac limousine.

The driver, in uniform, lounged against the rear fender.

Carter slipped him the keys as he passed. "Trunk. Plates are in beside the machine."

He spotted Ginger Bateman the moment he entered the diner, but no recognition passed between them. In the booth directly behind her sat Cole Lomax, a lower-level AXE operative.

Carter was barely two steps down the aisle when Lomax stood, slipped a dollar under his empty coffee mug, and left.

Carter slid into the booth and ordered a hearty breakfast. Ginger didn't speak until his coffee was served and the waitress had left.

"Done?"

"All done," Carter replied, leaning far back in the booth and speaking in a low voice.

"Any problems?"

"None. Your driver is getting the X-ray machine and plates from the trunk now."

"Good. Where to?"

"Boston . . . then an Air Canada flight to Toronto. I'll dump Petrovitch there and fly back to Boston as Harris-White."

Out of the corner of his eye he saw Ginger stretch. An instant later a key dropped onto the seat beside him.

"Your new bags are in that locker at Logan."

"Good enough. Do we have a pigeon in London yet?"

"Yes, an able-bodied seaman named Bijorn Lindeman.

He's a Swede, and he's trying to sign on as one of the crew that will sail Tejada's new yacht to Rio.''

"Good enough."

"Happy hunting."

Carter watched her tall, sleek figure move to the cash register to pay her bill. Two minutes after she exited, the Caddy limo pulled out onto the interstate and sped away.

As Devonovitch, Carter went through Canadian customs in a breeze. It was no more trouble than dumping Petrovitch's rented Chevrolet at Logan Airport in Boston.

He claimed the Russian's bag and his own small carry-on flight bag, then went directly to reservations and ticket sales at the British Airways counter.

"I believe you have a Frankfurt flight departing in fifty minutes," Carter said, passing across the passport and a credit card. "Have you space?"

"Yes, sir, Mr. . . . Devonovitch, we certainly do."

Carter paid for the tickets with a credit card and carefully signed the ticket.

"Any bags, sir?"

"Just these two. I'll carry the small black one."

"Fine."

"Oh . . . could I have my boarding pass now? I'd like to get a bite to eat."

"Certainly, sir. Smoking or nonsmoking?"

"Uh . . . smoking, please."

She was a pretty little brunette who smiled a lot. Carter kept Devonovitch's face grim and bored.

"There you are . . . a window seat."

"Thank you so much."

Little black bag in hand, Carter returned to the lobby and an out-of-the-way men's room near the baggage area.

He had to slip into a stall away from the mirrors twice while peeling away Devonovitch from his face.

Eventually he emerged from the restroom in a dark blue Savile Row suit. With a pencil-thin mustache, graying sideburns, and very prominent pouches under red-rimmed eyes, he looked like a very hung over but dapper British gentleman.

It took him only a minute or two to survey the long line in front of the ticket counter to pick out his mark.

The young man looked like a student: slightly long hair, a beard, and a backpack.

"Excuse me, lad . . . talk to you for a moment?"

"Sure."

"No, I mean over there . . . alone."

"Look, man, I'm not holding. They already searched me. Jesus, just because I got a beard—"

"Shh . . . shh, lad, nothing of the kind. I noticed the sticker on your small bag. Are you waiting in line to get a ticket on the British Airways flight to Frankfurt?"

"Yeah."

"Then come along, let's talk."

"Man, I'll lose my place in line!"

Carter smiled. "You'll gain much more."

He rubbed his thumb and index finger together. Money talks, even with fingers. The young man followed Carter to a nearby waiting area.

"Okay, what's the . . . ?"

Carter shoved the ticket into his hand.

"What's this?"

"Just what it looks like, son . . . a ticket on the flight you're about to take."

"So . . . ?"

Carter flipped the ticket booklet open. "So, read the price."

"Eight hundred and seventy-five dollars . . ."

"That's right. How would you like to own that ticket for three hundred?"

The ticket suddenly became very hot in the young man's hand. He quickly passed it back and started to move away. Carter quickly intercepted him.

"I assure you, it's genuine."

"Look, man, I don't wanna be scammed."

"No scam . . . real. Look, lad, I'm afraid I've got myself in a bit of trouble, a scramble last night in a bar. All my cash was lifted off me and I've got to pay a few people. I've wired my business partner for more money, but until it comes . . ."

The boy looked Carter up and down, then carefully examined the ticket.

"What about customs?"

Carter produced the boarding pass. "You've already gone through as me, Devonovitch, on this side. You can use your own passport on the other side to get out. Tell you what . . ."

"What?"

"Two hundred and fifty," Carter said, waving the boarding pass in front of the boy's face.

There was a scramble for a wallet, then a quick exchange of ticket, boarding pass, and money.

Seconds later, Carter was walking toward the gate for the Toronto to Boston flight, whistling a tuneless air.

But in his mind he was putting lyrics to it: "Petrovitch has disappeared, disappeared, disappeared. Petrovitch has disappeared, never seen no more-e-o!"

The tall, distinguished-looking man with the iron gray at the temples approached the Pan Am ticket counter at Boston's Logan Airport with a jaunty step, umbrella in hand, and a copy of the *Globe* under one arm.

"Good evening, my dear . . ." The accent was precise, clipped, very Oxford to the class-conscious ear of a fellow Britisher. "I believe you have a reservation and a ticket for Martin Harris-White? First Class, of course."

Fingers flew over computer keys, and seconds later she looked up with a beaming smile.

"Indeed, sir. One way, was it?"

"Yes."

"Could I see your passport, please?"

Carter handed her the United Kingdom passport and snapped his fingers toward the porter waiting nearby. "I'll be checking these three bags."

"Very good, sir."

Five minutes later, he settled into a lounge chair and began perusing the *Globe*.

He found it on page six:

AMALGAMATED REPORTER FOUND DEAD

Nicholas Carter, a long-time reporter for Amalgamated Press and Wire Services, was found dead early this morning in the charred shell of a cabin in upstate New York.

The victim of an accidental gas leak in the bedroom of the cabin, Mr. Carter's body was burned beyond recognition. Identification was eventually made with dental records provided by the Amalgamated offices.

An unidentified woman was also found in the cabin. As yet, authorities have been unable . . .

Carter barely scanned the rest of it. There was a rehash of his many years of service to Amalgamated and a quote of sadness from the wire service's operations officer, David Hawk.

Dropping the paper on a nearby seat, Carter lit a cigarette and mused to himself.

It was a pity people in his line of work couldn't keep a scrapbook.

How often was one able to paste one's own obituary in one's own scrapbook?

THREE

LONDON: SEVEN WEEKS BEFORE

London is a fantastic city in the summer, but its luster is somewhat dimmed in the dreary months of winter. Fog, chilling rain, and occasional gusts of bone-biting wind tend to keep even the whores of Soho alone between their warm sheets on particularly cold nights.

As the aristocratic British businessman Martin Harris-White, Carter checked into the Dorchester, put out the Do Not Disturb sign, and slept twelve hours.

The first order of business after waking was a call to his London contact. The contact would not know Carter, nor would he know anything about the operation.

All he would know was that he had orders from Washington three days before to put a twenty-four-hour surveillance on a Swedish seaman, Bijorn Lindeman.

"Amalgamated . . ."

"Jarvis Whitney, please."

Clicks, a few buzzes, and the young Englishman came on the line.

27

"Whitney here."

"Mr. Whitney, you have an appendectomy scar, and a mole just behind your right ear."

There was a moment's pause, during which Carter heard papers being shuffled. When the voice came on again, there was a touch of irritation in the tone.

"Highly irregular, this . . ."

"Mr. Whitney, what is regular or irregular is none of your concern. I believe you have a packet for me?"

"Yes, sir," came the swift reply. "It's waiting for you at the St. Paul's drop."

"Excellent. And our Mr. Lindeman?"

"His background is in the envelope along with the other information."

"And the photos?"

"Ten of them."

"Current address and habits?"

"Everything," Whitney replied. "You know the method of pickup?"

"Quite well, Mr. Whitney. You may pull your men off the surveillance at once."

"Very well, but . . ."

"No buts, Mr. Whitney. Good day."

Carter showered, dressed, and took the elevator to the lobby. He had a scotch in the lobby lounge and treated himself to a sumptuous meal in the Dorchester's ornate dining room.

It was just eight-thirty when he stepped into a cab in front of the hotel.

"St. Paul's."

"Right you are, sir."

There was hardly any traffic, but the fog was rolling in. It lengthened the usual fifteen-minute ride to near thirty.

It was one minute after nine when Carter strolled across St. Paul's common. The old man at the newsstand was just closing up shop, idly chatting to a bobbie as he worked.

Carter waited until he could wait no more.

"I say . . ."

"Good evening, sir," the bobbie said, touching the stick he held to the short bill of his helmet. "It's a bloody night."

"Indeed it is," Carter replied. "Saw a bit of a fuss over there, just now, right off the Paternoster Square. Hooligans, perhaps."

"Right-o, have a look, I will. Evenin' to ya, Thorny . . . sir."

The bobbie's heels resounded even after his figure receded into the fog.

"Somethin' fer ya, sir?"

"Yes," Carter replied. "I believe you have a packet for me."

"Do I, now?"

"Yes. Manila envelope, thirteen by fifteen, stapled across the top, no markings."

"I might."

"The envelope," Carter said, laying three bills in the old man's hand, "is worth exactly thirty pounds."

The old man scurried behind the racks of newspapers and magazines. In an instant he was back, a copy of the *Times* in his hand. It bulged slightly in the middle.

Carter took the paper and, without a word, strolled into the fog.

Two blocks along, he doubled the envelope, slid it into his inside coat pocket, and started looking for a pub.

He rejected two establishments as too full and rowdy. A third, The Raven's Wing, was perfect: a long, occupied bar, and four empty booths in the rear.

Carter slid into the last one and ordered. "A pint, please."

He paid the buxom barmaid with a pound note and waved the change away. She was hardly halfway back to the bar before Carter was perusing the contents of the envelope.

There was a complete rundown on the *Excalibur*. It was quite a boat, 175 feet of seagoing luxury.

It had been purchased two months before by a private company in Liechtenstein from a Middle Eastern sheik who had deemed it too small for his use.

Right now it was in the Cheltenham yards being completely refitted from stem to stern for delivery to the government of Brazil. The *Excalibur* was to be rechristened *Lapita* and was, like its namesake, Lapita del Preda, destined to be the personal toy of President Frederico Tejada.

Carter glanced on down the sheet and smiled when he saw the delivery date.

AXE intelligence in South America was on the ball.

He resheathed the yacht information in the manila envelope and withdrew the assembled file on Bijorn Lindeman.

Bijorn was quite a boy. Under four different aliases, he was wanted in Brussels, Amsterdam, and Stockholm for everything from smuggling to murder.

While his record at sea as a machinist was good, Lindeman couldn't seem to stay out of trouble on dry land. The man's personality profile met every requirement Carter had set up.

Lindeman was the kind of man who would always be a failure. He was constantly looking for the brass ring, the

one big score, rather than grabbing the little, easier pick-
ings and running.

Carter took a rubber band from around the photos and
spread them on the table before him.

The face that stared back at him was lean and badly in
need of a shave. The lips were thin, and the eyes seemed
glazed behind cynically drooping lids. On his right cheek
was an ugly, purplish scar, and beneath a woolen seaman's cap strands of dirty blond hair hung limply over his
ears.

The physical description was six-feet-one.

Good. Only an inch off, and the build was almost
identical to his own.

Carter smiled as he shoved the envelope and its contents
back into his coat.

Lindeman's face was the best part. It would be a piece
of cake to duplicate.

He checked his watch.

It was eleven-thirty.

He would just make his second appointment of the
evening at midnight.

Carter rang the tiny bell and tapped the steel tip of his
umbrella against the concrete of the stoop while he
waited.

"Yes?"

"Monsieur Claude DuPugh?"

"Yes . . . it is very late."

"My name is Harris-White. I sent you a wire . . ."

"Yes, yes . . . come in."

He was a squat, round man with spindly legs and a
gleaming bald pate surrounded by gray fuzz.

Carter followed him through a large room filled with

radios, stereos, televisions, and other electronic machinery in various states of repair and disrepair.

In a small cubicle that appeared to serve the dual purposes of office and living quarters, the old man turned on a low, overhead hanging lamp and locked the door.

"My acquaintances in Ulster send their regards. You have done a great deal for their cause."

"I care less than shit for causes . . . yours, theirs, or anyone else's," the old man growled. "I work for my retirement."

"Nevertheless, they recommend you highly."

"They should. My devices always work. Now, what is it you wish?"

Carter unfolded a sheet of paper and spread it on the table. On it, drawn to scale by a master draftsman, were the working drawings for the device he would need to eventually complete the mission.

"This was laid out and drawn by an expert. You?"

"No," Carter replied, "a member of my group."

Carter lit a cigarette and leaned back in his chair as the old man adjusted his spectacles and perused the plan that had originally been conceived and drawn up in the basement of the Amalgamated Building on Dupont Circle.

The AXE specialists could have easily built the device, but then too many people would have been privy to the mission.

"No U.S. involvement," Hawk had said, and that meant that not a stitch of clothing or remnant of an explosive device could be traceable.

It took the old man a good half hour to digest the full content and the intricacies of the plan. But when he looked up, Carter felt as though he understood it completely . . . perhaps even memorized it.

"It is very involved."

"I understand that," Carter replied.

"And the explosive device will have to be calibrated exactly to the detonator. Must the detonator be housed in this rocket affair?"

"Unless you can construct a beam-in that will calibrate to the second from a distance of six miles . . . perhaps more."

The old man frowned and scratched his bald head. "No, impossible, if the distance is that great."

"And," Carter added, "the bomb itself must be no larger than the specifications call for."

"That means plastique . . ."

"I thought as much."

"That much plastique, cored, will be very expensive."

"So be it," Carter replied, pulling a thick envelope from his inside jacket pocket. "Half now, half upon delivery."

"And half is . . . ?" the old man asked, eyeing the envelope but not touching it.

"Ten thousand pounds. I shall need the explosive device, the transmitter, and the detonator by a week from today."

"That will be very difficult."

"Then shall we say a thousand-pound bonus. A week from today . . . about this same time?"

The old man smiled for the first time since the conversation had begun. "I think *two* thousand pounds will make the wheels of progress turn very quickly."

Carter cabbed back to the Dorchester and stopped at the telegram desk in the lobby.

To: D.F. Pause
      12 W. 9th St.
      NY NY

From: Martin Harris-White
        Dorchester
        London, England
        W1

    Dear Uncle David . . . Progress on new orders at maximum . . . Please advise Latin buyer ETA Paris.

Martin

"Could you still get this off tonight, miss?"

"Of course . . . your room number, sir?"

Carter gave her the room number, paid, adding an extra two pounds, and took the elevator to his room.

In the little black bag, he carefully stored all the accouterments that he would use to transform himself the next evening into Salvatore Bellini.

When this was done, he extracted Willie Geis's master makeup kit from one of the large bags and spread its contents out on the dressing table. Along the mirror he propped up the ten snapshots of Bijorn Lindeman.

For the next several hours, he worked intently in front of the mirror with false hair, shading pencil, spirit gum, latex, and assorted mastics to expand his nostrils and jowls.

It was dawn by the time he was completely satisfied that the face staring back at him from the mirror was Bijorn Lindeman.

Into the bag went the necessary makeup to again reproduce the Swede, along with a tiny tape recorder.

When the face was scrubbed clean and the Do Not Disturb sign was again in place, he crawled into the bed.

In five seconds he was dreamlessly asleep.

The streets and pubs beneath Duke Street Hill on the south side of the Thames had been the nests and haunts of the scum of London during the time of Queen Elizabeth I.

They hadn't changed much.

Pimps, thieves, whores, and cutthroats—and others aspiring to those professions—roamed like hungry alley cats in the tiny byways.

The sounds, sights, and smells of a teeming London met Carter as he paid the taxi driver near the foot of Southwark Bridge.

"I'd have a mind to it, round 'ere this time 'a night, mate."

"Eh," Carter shrugged. "Who'd'a wanna hurt an old'a man like me?"

"Anybody who thinks ya might have a quid in yer pocket, mate."

The taxi roared away, and Carter began walking.

As Harris-White he had been here earlier in the afternoon, so he already knew the route.

Then, of course, he had clipped along with the brisk stride of the dapper English gentleman Harris-White was.

But now he was Salvatore Bellini, a shambling, rotund man with fleshy jowls and a "mustache Pete" face. His shoulders were rounded, and the wide brim of his black hat nearly touched his back, giving the appearance that he had no neck.

He passed the water side of Southwark Cathedral and walked down into the narrow, grimy streets of Southwark itself.

The yellow lamps of the streetlights fought valiantly with the fog, but it was a losing battle.

He rounded a corner, away from the river, and nearly crashed into a young woman.

"Pardon, *signorina*."

"S'okay, dearie . . . ya lookin' fer a date?"

"N-no, thank you."

"Name's Fancy, luv."

"Good night, Fancy . . ."

"Aw, come on, luv . . . it's only five quid. Let's see what ya got!"

Her hand was slow reaching for his crotch, far too slow. Carter gripped her wrist, turned her around bodily, and lifted her two feet off the ground with his knee.

"I'm an old man, girl, and you should be ashamed of yourself."

His gentle nudge dropped her against a wall five feet away. Her face went white as she edged away from him.

"B'damn, ye're a mean 'un, ain't ya!"

But Carter was already slouching along a quarter of a block away. It was three more blocks to his destination, and in that space he was propositioned twice more and eyed closely by three teenage toughs.

The teenagers were quickly discouraged when he waved a friendly greeting to them and his right hand filled with a stiletto.

They were gone into the fog the instant they saw light flash on Hugo's blade.

A rusty, yellowing sign swinging on a creaky chain proclaimed The Mariner.

Inside, it was one vast, sprawling room. It had a bar down one side and another on a raised platform in the rear. The stools of both bars were filled with an assortment of

toughs and tarts that, had they been in the proper costume,
could have stepped right into the England of King Henry
VIII.

Tables filled the center of the room, and rough-hewn,
scarred wooden booths lined one wall. Most of these were
filled as well with seamen, more women, and gnarled old
men.

The Mariner was not unlike a hundred waterfront bars
Carter had been in all over the world. He guessed that
every hour on the hour, recreation in the restroom con-
sisted of a few eye gouges and some broken arms and
legs.

Carter spotted his prey at once in one of the wall booths.
He was dressed in a pair of dungarees, a frayed pea jacket,
and an open-necked shirt. Beneath the shirt, wiry blond
hair carpeted his chest practically to the center of his neck.
Above that, his face sprouted a five-day growth of blond
beard speckled with a little gray.

All eyes cased the rotund little Italian-looking man as
he entered, including Lindeman's hazy blue orbs. Like the
others, the Swede checked Carter, dismissed him, and
moved back to the aging whore beside him.

She was a tired-looking, blowsy redhead whose
breasts, shelved on the table before her, threatened to
dwarf the mug of beer between them.

She had her good years behind her, and it was in
Lindeman's eyes as he looked at her. She, on the other
hand, looked at him as if the Swede were a life jacket and
she was drowning.

The setup was perfect.

Carter ambled to the bar and squeezed his padded bulk
onto a stool in between two oldsters.

"What'll ya have, mate?"

"A glass of red wine, please."

The barman and everyone within ten feet roared with laughter.

"Mate, ye'll have beer or gin an' bitters. It's all we got."

"A pint of your best then."

The pint came. Carter sprinkled some coins on the counter and nodded at the squinty-eyed little man beside him.

"Eye-talian, is it?"

"Yes."

"I don't like Eye-talians, I don't."

"My mother was English."

"Then I don't like haf' of ya."

Carter only smiled, sipped his pint, and glanced now and then approvingly at the redhead with Lindeman. When the Swede left the table for the john, Carter stepped up the process, and so did she.

When Lindeman came back, she spoke to him hurriedly behind a cupped hand. His pale blue eyes darted up to Carter as she spoke, and then he was nodding in agreement.

"Mate, I told ya I don't like haf' of ya."

Carter, still smiling, leaned close to the old man. "Mate, I really don't give a shit. Now, suppose you move to another stool—I'm about to have company."

The squinty eyes went wide when Carter emphasized his words by pouring his pint of beer into the old man's lap. He slipped from the stool and creaked into a fighting pose that made him look like a bantam rooster trying to imitate John L. Sullivan.

Again Carter leaned forward, oblivious to the man's cocked right fist. "If you swing on me, old man, I'll break your arm. If you don't move then, I'll put your balls alongside your Adam's apple with my foot.''

There was more raucous laughter, and the old man moved on down the bar muttering, ''Damn Eye-talians.''

The redhead moved onto the unoccupied stool.

''Evenin' . . . buy a lady a drink?''

''Another pint for me, please, and a gin and bitters for the lady.''

There was more laughter from the drinkers nearby at the word ''lady,'' and Carter knew it was clear sailing for the night.

In a bar like The Mariner, guts meant everything, even when they were exhibited against an old man by a paunchy Italian.

''Would you be lookin' fer a date, luv?''

''Perhaps.''

''They have nice cozy rooms upstairs, they 'ave . . . only five quid and a few bob tip fer the woman who cleans.''

Carter put his arm around her thickening middle, and together they slid off the stools. ''Lead the way, my dear.''

''Don't ya wanna know me price?'' she whispered.

''For you, price can be no object.''

''My, my, yer a gent, you are!''

Carter didn't miss the high sign she gave Lindeman as they passed the table. Nor did he miss the Swede's hand tap the shoulder of a swarthy, bull-like man in the booth behind him.

The room was utilitarian at best: a chair, a bedside stand with a wash basin and one dirty towel, and a bed.

''It'll be in advance, luv . . . five quid fer the room, and . . . uh, twenty fer me.''

"Twenty? I thought ten would be plenty."

"Ah, now, luv, ain't a bit of a roll with these worth twenty?"

She parted the front of her dress, and two braless mountains of dark-tipped flesh tumbled through the opening.

"Twenty it is," Carter said, pulling a thick wad of notes from his pocket.

He peeled off a twenty and a five, and placed them in her hand. Her eyes were so wide with shock and greed that she was paying no attention to the two bills, only to the thick wad in his other hand.

"You get undressed, luv. I'll have to pay fer the room."

"You do that."

She didn't even stuff her breasts back into the dress as she hurried from the room.

Carter moved to the side of the door so he'd be behind it when it opened, pulled Wilhelmina from the small of his back, flipped her so that the barrel was in his hand, and waited.

It wasn't long, less than two minutes.

The big, dark-skinned man slammed through the door first, with Lindeman close behind him. The Swede went to the right. The big man stood near the foot of the bed, the sap in his right hand hovering to strike.

The butt of the Luger made a sharp crack against the back of his skull, and his body sounded like a felled oak thudding against the bare floor.

Carter kicked the door shut and flipped the gun butt into his palm. In the same movement, he shoved the Luger's ugly snout into the Swede's neck.

"Bijorn Lindeman?"

"Who the hell . . . ?"

"My name doesn't matter, but it's Bellini . . . Salvatore Bellini."

"You move fast for a fat man, Bellini."

"Sit down . . . there!" Carter ordered, gesturing with his free hand.

"Up your friggin' . . ."

Carter's backhand caught him flush on the side of the head, sending him sprawling over the bed.

"I am much quicker and stronger than I look, Signore Lindeman. Now please sit quietly and listen to what I have to say."

"You a copper?" Lindeman asked, shaking the bells from his head.

"No."

"Then how do ya know my name?"

"I know a great deal about you, Bijorn Lindeman. You are an ex-convict wanted in three different countries. You are in England now with false papers, but you are trying to bribe your way into a berth aboard the yacht *Lapita*, which sails for Rio in ten days."

"By God . . ."

Carter took the wad of bills from his pocket and dropped it on the bed. The Swede's eyes watered.

"There is more than enough there to make the bribe. Next week we will meet again. I will give you a package that must go to Rio aboard the *Lapita*."

Lindeman's cracked lips broke into a smile, showing crooked brown teeth.

This was the kind of talk he understood.

"How much?"

"Ten thousand goes with the package, another ten thousand in Rio."

"Thirty," came the quick reply. "Fifteen here, fifteen there."

The heel of Carter's left hand came out like a striking snake. Beneath it, the cartilage in Lindeman's nose shattered like jelly. Blood spilled over his lips as Carter squeezed his cheeks. With the Swede's mouth opened wide, Carter shoved three inches of the Luger's barrel between his teeth.

A cry of agony erupted from the man's throat as the gun ripped flesh from the roof of his mouth.

"Salvatore Bellini is not a man who barters or argues, Signore Lindeman. Nod if you understand."

Lindeman nodded.

"If you don't wish to accept my offer, I will blow the back of your head off and find someone else to deliver my package. Nod if you understand!"

Bijorn Lindeman nodded . . . and nodded . . . and nodded.

Indeed, he was still nodding when the rotund Italian walked from the room.

An hour later, Carter stepped through the Dorchester's revolving doors and moved to the desk.

"My key, please."

"Yes, sir . . . oh, Mr. Harris-White, there's a telegram for you, sir."

"Thank you."

Carter read it in the elevator.

Dear Martin:

Your Latin buyer arrived in Paris this morning. Staying at the Crillon, Suite 900. Do call home when you return to London. Must tell you about a new

wrinkle in the competition.
Uncle David.

Two hours later Carter was on the night train to Dover
with a through ticket to Calais and Paris.

FOUR

RIO: NOW

Carter strolled leisurely, rolling his padded paunch along the Avenida Rio Branco as if he had no thoughts beyond a morning walk and no destination. Only his eyes—darting, seeing everything he passed—gave a hint that there was anything on his mind beyond a morning stroll.

The Avenida Rio Branco ran the full length of the city, from the Rio equivalent of Wall Street, past the posh Leme residential district, and above beautiful Copacabana Beach. It was a block-wide street, its colorful mosaic sidewalks now filled with people alive with the new day.

Flower sellers, shoeshine stands, and exclusive boutiques melded with cafeterias and bars. Near the formal gardens of the Beira Mar, he left the avenue and turned inward, away from the bay, onto a tiny, narrow street filled with cafés and bistros.

Eventually he stopped beneath a sign reading Café Swiss.

The tables on the sidewalk were crowded with break-fasters. Inside, only two tables were occupied: one with a family of three, and several tables away in a corner, a lone woman.

She was a handsome woman with sleek, dark hair tightly coiled at the nape of her neck. When she glanced up, her coal-black eyes smoldered deeply in her olive-skinned, oval face.

Her eyes barely glanced at the round Italian before dancing down the street in search of someone else.

Carter weaved his way awkwardly through the sidewalk tables and entered the interior.

"A table, *senhor*?"

"*Sim*, but I prefer inside, please."

The waiter smiled with appreciation at the man's perfect Portuguese. "This way, sir."

Carter was seated two tables away from the woman. He ordered coffee and breakfast. Just before the waiter stepped away, Carter grasped his arm.

"Pardon . . ."

"*Sim?*"

"Isn't that Senhorita Braz, daughter of the Minister of Commerce?"

"*Sim.*"

"I thought so. I must pay my respects. Bring my coffee to her table."

"*Sim, senhor.*"

Carter waddled the distance between the two tables with his hands on his paunch, one thumb stroking a gold medallion in the watch pocket of his vest.

"Senhorita Braz?"

"*Sim?*"

As agitated as she was, her face still had the serenity and the beauty of a madonna when she looked up toward him. Carter resisted the impulse to run his fingers along the firm line of her strong jaw.

"Senhorita Braz, I wish to tell you how much your father has helped our government . . ."

"Thank you."

"I wonder if I might sit down . . ."

"Uh . . . I am very sorry, but I am expecting someone."

Shielding the movement from the eyes of the other diners with his body, Carter flipped the medallion from his vest and swung it slowly in his fingers.

"I know, *senhorita*," he said, his pulpy face breaking into a wide smile.

She narrowed her eyes, recognized the medallion, and gasped. "He sent you . . . the Englishman?" she asked in a low whisper.

"No, Leonora, I am he," Carter replied and slipped into the booth beside her.

Another, much louder gasp.

"Shhh, control yourself."

"Your coffee, *senhor*."

"*Obrigado*," Carter replied. When the waiter was gone, he turned back to face Leonora Braz.

The look in her wide eyes and the way her hands gripped each other in her lap said worlds.

"You're wondering how this overweight, florid-faced Italian could be the same tall Englishman you loved so passionately less than a week ago . . ."

Her dark complexion lightened at least two shades, blushed, and then her eyes dropped to her lap.

"Of course I am. Is there any *real* you? You have been a Brazilian, an Englishman, and now an—"

"Italian. Salvatore Bellini. It's all part of doing the job, Leonora."

"Oh? And was . . . ?" She stopped to bring her hands to her cup and the cup to her face to hide her frustration.

". . . making love to you? No, that was just a very lucky thing that happened to me, quite by chance. And believe me when I say that it was an accident, not planned in any way."

Her eyes when she lifted them to his were misty, but there was a slight smile on her lips. "I believe you."

"Good. Now, to business. Your father has made the arrangements for his own safety?"

"Yes."

"And Captain Ortez, he is ready to take the airfield?"

She nodded. "We received word about an hour ago. He and his men are in place."

"And the tanker? . . . It will be on time?"

"According to our intelligence it will sail into the bay at the precise moment of your estimation."

"Then, if your father's rebel forces under Miguel Orantes are in place around the city, the government should be in Luís Braz's hands by this evening."

Suddenly she turned to face him, her dark, limpid eyes wide with emotion. "Do you really think this can be done? . . . I mean, can one man single-handedly overthrow a government?"

Carter smiled. "I am not one man, remember? I am many. And besides, you, your father, and his followers have done much of the work."

Her hands left the tabletop and one of them moved to rest on his leg. "Who are you . . . really?"

"Leonora, I am a man who seizes opportunity. Why? For money."

"No, there must be more."

"There isn't," he hissed. "Don't deceive yourself. I

am no more than a mercenary soldier selling my mind and body to the highest bidder.''

"No, I won't believe that . . .''

A tear squeezed from the corner of one eye. She wiped it away and stared intently into his face.

Carter hated to hit her when she was down, but he had to. It had been a mistake making love to her. Now he had to convince her that he didn't even exist, that he was a myth.

"You'll have to believe it. Your country means nothing to me . . . your money does.''

"Then that means that, one day, you could come back and destroy my father as you are destroying the others now.''

"Yes,'' he said and nodded, "I could. Now . . . the helicopter will be waiting?''

"Yes.'' The grimness that Carter had been hoping for had finally crept into her voice.

"Then there is only one last thing . . .''

"The money.''

"The money,'' he repeated.

"The amount you asked for is there in that briefcase along with the other things. Here is the telexed deposit slip from the account you named in the Cayman Islands. The remainder, my father will give you just before your departure . . . if you survive.''

Carter smiled. "I will survive, Leonora. We all will. And the passport?''

"Done, along with the money.'' She slid the deposit slip and a separate piece of paper with the required figures across the table.

Carter examined them all carefully and suppressed the sigh of relief he felt. It had been a very expensive operation, too expensive for AXE to account for without revealing the nature of the mission.

But now that wouldn't be necessary.

Brazil had paid for its own revolution.

"I'll be going now, and I do hope your father hasn't anyone lurking around to follow me."

"No. Your instructions have been followed to the letter."

He started to slide from the booth, but her fingers gripped his sleeve.

"I'll never see you again, will I?"

"No. And even if you did, you wouldn't—or couldn't—know me. *Adeus*, Leonora."

Carter moved into the sunlight without looking back.

His eyes searched the square of the Praça do Coro for the shaggy blond head, much as they had scanned the smokey depths of The Mariner pub in London weeks earlier.

Then he saw him, slouched, beady eyes scanning every passerby, the unkempt blond hair framing his heavy, piglike face.

He slowly approached the tall Swede, studying the intent look of anticipation when he was recognized.

Good, very good, Carter thought. *The greedy bastard is even more anxious for the final payment than he was for the deposit*.

Beyond the Swede and the statues lining the square, he could see the arches of Bilbao Station. Somewhere beyond those arches they would be waiting: dark-suited, eager, deadly.

General Fernandes couldn't afford to let the Swede out of the country. He couldn't live with the fact that, somewhere in the world, another man knew that the death of

President Frederico Tejada was an assassination.

They would kill the Swede at once. And if they didn't, Luís Braz's man would.

Carter had thought of everything.

He hoped.

Fernandes was ruthless as well as shrewd, but not shrewd enough. He would never inspect the body, nor would he speak to the Swede alive. Therefore, he would never connect the somewhat cultured, obviously educated coconspirator he'd met in Paris with the real Bijorn Lindeman . . . a man of no education, little criminal talent, and an ex-convict turned merchant seaman to escape the police of his native country.

Braz's man, if he were Lindeman's executioner, wouldn't care.

"Signore Bellini."

"Sit, sit! *Come sta*, my friend?" He took a place beside the Swede and smiled benevolently at the square. "It is a fine day. How goes your heart today, Bijorn?"

"Am scared, I am."

"No need, my friend. Your delivery was punctual . . . as is mine now."

"Small package for so much money."

"Highly expensive things often come in small packages, Bijorn. You did place the package exactly as I instructed you from the ship's floor plan?"

"Yes, on the catwalk above the diesels, just under the flying bridge."

Carter leered and squinted his eyes as he leaned his face close to the other man's. "I hope you did, Bijorn, because if it isn't there at four this afternoon, I shall come looking for you."

From the sweat breaking out immediately on the Swede's face, Carter knew he was remembering London and three inches of Wilhelmina down his throat.

"I did," he choked. "I put it there. But now I think I'm just as afraid of these crazy people as I am of you."

Carter laughed. "You should be, my friend. Many of them are very unstable."

"So, what was in the package?"

"Do you really care, Bijorn? You've smuggled everything from diamonds to dope and have never been paid near what I've paid you."

A dark-eyed beauty with large, jutting breasts in a low-cut peasant blouse jiggled across the path in front of them.

"*Fantastico*. Sad, what age does to one," Carter mused.

"Age ain't gonna be no problem when I get my hands on my money. It's in here?"

His hand reached for the briefcase, only to be stopped in mid-move. The grip on his wrist was like that of the jaws of a timber wolf—ten, even a hundred times stronger than he would have given the old man credit for.

"First things first, my friend." Carter released the Swede's hand and then filled it with an envelope. "There is your passport, visa, tickets, and all other papers you'll need. I want you to know, losing your passport was stupid. Getting another was very difficult."

"It was taken! Somebody nipped it right from my room!"

"Stupid, nevertheless. But no matter. It's taken care of."

The Swede quickly rifled through the papers and stowed them in his jacket. "What's in the case besides the money?"

The round man's lips curved into a jeering smile. "You've been double-crossing people so long, Bijorn, you can't trust anybody."

"No, no . . . look, I'm sorry."

"Just clothes and a few toilet articles. The money, as I promised, is in pounds. It is between two layers of leather lining the whole case. Here!"

He pushed the case toward the other man with his foot. The Swede's eyes glinted as he grabbed for it greedily and hoisted it to his lap. There he covered it and rocked it like a newborn babe.

Carter stood. "I will be going now."

"Yes, good. Was a pleasure doin' business with you, Signore Bellini."

Carter turned away from the crafty, smiling Swede, and headed across the square.

The bells of Candelária tolled the time.

In a little more than seven hours, Bijorn Lindeman would be a dead man.

FIVE

PARIS: SIX WEEKS BEFORE

General Pablo Fernandes stepped from the shower and stretched in the luxury of the enormous Crillon bath.

And then he frowned.

They were waiting, three of them, in the adjoining suite: one Iranian, one Russian, and one Libyan.

They were waiting to see him, but he was only the lackey, the voice of President Frederico Tejada.

He could still hear their whispered, individual comments as they filed from the room at the conclusion of the previous day's meeting.

"Ah, General, it is a pity that you are not the president. With the recent, unexpected discovery of vast, offshore oil fields in your country, we would make you a very powerful ally . . . *very* powerful indeed."

It was true.

With the Russians behind him, he could stave off American intervention and reap the profits of the new oil for himself . . . as Tejada was about to do.

He could do it if he were Brazil's president.

But he wasn't. He knew it, and they knew it. And there was very little chance of him obtaining the office as long as Tejada was alive.

And there was even less chance that Tejada would die.

Fernandes dried his body and gazed through the open door at Cecília's youthful, nude body on the bed. She was eighteen now. She had been his mistress since the age of fifteen.

That was one thing he had that Tejada didn't have: a young, beautiful, and vibrant mistress. Tejada's whore, Lapita del Preda, was pushing forty, with sagging breasts and tired hips.

Cecília hadn't moved since they had finished. His residue was still visible in the darkness between her thighs.

Fernandes chuckled silently to himself. What would the three very important men from the three very important countries say if they knew that they had been kept waiting two hours because he, Fernandes, had gotten a sudden urge to taste the sweet sex of his mistress's voluptuous body?

"Cecília?"

"Yes?"

"My uniform."

She brought his clothes to him not like a puppy or a servant but like a loyal follower who considered Fernandes's every command and desire—no matter how small—weighty and important.

She kissed him lightly and returned to the bed. He watched her. She had a marvelous, firm ass that rippled with each step rather than jiggled. She kept her body tuned like the engine of an expensive car; she was always willing, always able, to drive his own body to exalted heights of erotic glee.

Fernandes dressed and surveyed himself in a mirror. He looked good in uniform, far better than he had in the rags of his youth. He wore clothes well on his huge frame. Far from lean, he was an enormous man, but at fifty there was not an ounce of excess fat anywhere on him.

"Cecília?"

There was no answer.

Angrily, Fernandes called again. When there was still no answer, he charged from the bath into the bedroom, only to stop short with a sudden growl.

Cecília lay sprawled grotesquely across the bed.

Sitting in a chair by the window was a tall, ugly man with a scarred face and a tangled mane of dirty blond hair. He was dressed in the scarlet and blue livery of the Crillon's army of bellmen.

"Who are . . . ?"

"My name is Bijorn Lindeman, General, and I fear I don't have an appointment."

Fernandes's narrow eyes flicked to Cecília on the bed. "Is she dead?"

"No."

"João! . , . Guilherme . . . !"

"Are they the two bodyguards I found lurking like puppies outside your door, General?"

"They are . . ."

"They are, like your woman, sleeping peacefully," the man said, brandishing a large cotton wad in one hand.

The general sniffed the air.

Chloroform.

Again his eyes went to the bed but this time going to the holstered .38 service revolver hanging over the bedpost.

"Don't even think about it, General. I could kill you in half a devil's minute." To prove his point, the man produced a Luger with a long, ugly silencer attached to its snout. "And that, believe me, I do not want to do."

Pablo Fernandes was sweating. He could feel beads of perspiration popping from the pores on his forehead as well as a steady stream trickling down the center of his back.

The general was not a man who frightened easily. But there was something deadly, a little bit crazy, about this man. It was in the expressionless eyes that stared like tiny chunks of pale blue ice from his gaunt face. It was also in the careless yet expert way he handled and caressed the Luger.

Fernandes did not know who this man was or what he wanted, but he sensed that the intruder was as deadly as he looked and sounded.

He decided to play for time.

"Lindeman, is it?"

"Bijorn Lindeman," the man replied, nodding, "but the name means little."

"Very well, Lindeman, if you are not an assassin, what do you want?"

The thin lips twisted into one of the coldest, most evil smiles Fernandes had ever seen.

"I didn't say I wasn't an assassin, General. I just said I wasn't going to assassinate you."

From beneath the scarlet uniform jacket he took a thick envelope and tossed it on the bed.

"I want you to read that, General."

"Now see here," Fernandes blustered, "I have some very important men waiting for me in my other suite . . ."

"You did have."

"Good God, you didn't drug them too, did you?"

"No. I merely told them that you had a serious attack of indigestion. All this rich Crillon food." He paused, waving the Luger around the room. "They will return at six o'clock."

"You have gall, I'll give you that."

"Yes, I do," Lindeman agreed. Again that chilling, icy smile. "Open the envelope, General. Make yourself comfortable . . . and read the papers."

Fernandes lifted the envelope from the bed and broke the seal.

"This is over two hundred pages!" he exclaimed riffling through them.

"It is a very elaborate plan."

"A plan? For what?"

"A plan, General Fernandes, to make you the president of Brazil."

It was ten minutes past six when General Pablo Fernandes stepped into the conference suite.

They were waiting, all three of them.

He grooved a smile onto his thick, almost cruel lips, and moved toward the table where the three men sat.

"Forgive me, gentlemen. Forgive me for keeping such important guests waiting. I had business that could not be diverted."

The three stood, nodding their mute acceptance and returning Fernandes's bow. Their faces wore patient expressions, but inside, Fernandes knew they were seething.

Let them, he thought. *They will seethe more at my news*.

He snapped his fingers, and a servant supplied fresh drinks all around. The three regained their seats, and Fernandes sat at the mouth of the horseshoe they formed.

After general amenities had been observed, Fernandes lit a cigar and leaned back in his chair.

"Gentlemen, this meeting was initially called to discuss the purchase from your respective countries—or the funneling through your countries—of arms for my government."

The three heads nodded.

"But in the past we have had other, shall we say, more *clandestine* discussions about the future of my country."

Again the three heads nodded.

Fernandes leaned forward now, his voice low and husky, as he outlined a plan that was brilliant in its audacity.

When he was finished, the three men sat stunned.

One by one they spoke.

"Is it possible?"

"It has elements of genius."

"Could we have a brief conference?"

Fernandes smiled as he leaned back and watched them retreat to a far corner of the room where they stood with their heads together.

He would need them after the coup, perhaps for some time, to ward off American intervention.

But when their usefulness was over. . . .

As one, they returned to the table.

"General, we congratulate you."

Fernandes smiled and snapped his fingers.

Beyond the men, the door opened at the far end of the room and Cecília stepped through. She carried a tray holding five glasses of poured champagne.

Fernandes stood.

He was pleased. She was a vision of sultry loveliness. She had worn the white dress that accented the olive glory of her skin and dark richness of her satiny black hair. It hugged her round hips and full thighs like a second skin. The front of the dress was cut low and draped open to amply reveal the jutting fullness of her breasts. On each side there was the barest hint of a darker nipple.

Her appearance more than captivated the attention of the three men around the table as she served the champagne.

When all the glasses had been passed out, Cecília stood at the head of the table and raised her own.

"Gentlemen, a toast. To the creation of the next president of Brazil, General Pablo Fernandes."

Carter set his bags beside the phone booth, entered, and closed the door to the bustle and noise of Heathrow Airport.

It took him a full two minutes to make contact with an overseas operator.

"Yes, I would like to place a person-to-person call to D. F. Pause in Washington, D.C., please."

"The number?"

Carter gave the woman Hawk's ultraprivate number. "Collect, please."

"Whom shall I say is calling?"

"His nephew."

"Yes, sir, one moment."

It took almost four minutes to complete the call. By the time Carter had inserted a small scrambler into the mouthpiece on his end of the line, Hawk's voice was rumbling on the other end.

"Yes, yes, operator, I'll accept the call."

"Go ahead, please."

"Uncle David?"

"Yes, my boy."

Carter pushed the button on the scrambler and heard Hawk do the same. When the whirrs and buzzes died down to a roar, Hawk spoke again.

"How goes it there?"

"Good, so far. The device is completed, and Lindeman

has his half of it. The rest is in my bags.''

''Are you sure it will work?''

''Positive,'' Carter replied. ''Claude DuPugh is a genius. We really should take him out of circulation.''

''His time will come. And Paris?''

''I established the Swede with Fernandes, and the general is firmly convinced that he is the next president of Brazil. In return, he was only too happy to sign the false OPEC agreement I presented.''

Hawk chuckled. ''And which, if he did become president, he would promptly tear up and bring in the Russians.''

''No doubt of it. He met with their people less than an hour after I left him.''

''It sounds as though you're done there then.''

''I am,'' Carter replied. ''I'm at Heathrow now.''

''Then I'm glad you made contact before your flight. Things have altered.''

''Oh?''

''Tejada has refused to come to Washington. He's requested a secret meet with his CIA liaison in Miami instead.''

''Wants more CIA money to prop up his government,'' Carter growled.

''Probably. But there's not a lot State can do about it as long as he's the power.'' Hawk chuckled again, and Carter could almost see a leer of satisfaction spread across the old man's face when he spoke again. ''But then, that's why you're on the mission you're on.''

''So it's Miami?''

''Day after tomorrow,'' Hawk replied. ''The CIA man is Brandon Hall. He's a good man, very sharp, so you'll have to be twice as sharp to fool him.''

''And Moncada?''

"He was a for-real lieutenant for Tejada years ago. He died in one of the president's secret purges. It's a pretty sure thing Tejada never heard of him, let alone that he knew him personally."

"What about records?" Carter asked.

"Our people down there have managed to lift all traces of Moncada from Rio and the capital. He did most of his duty—when he was alive—in a small southern province, so it will be hard for Tejada's intelligence people to come up with anything on him."

"Making it hard to prove that Moncada is not for real, or even dead."

"Right," Hawk said. "If you've got the plan for the coup and the agreement signed by Fernandes, and if you're convincing enough as Moncada, both the president and Hall should buy the deal."

"How influential is Brandon Hall?"

"So-so. His job is to keep the lid on Tejada as much as possible and report to State if he has trouble doing it. Let's face it, the Tejada regime hasn't been exactly noted for observing human rights. All Hall can do is try to advise the egomaniac and inform State if he goes too far."

"I'll catch the next Miami flight," Carter said.

"Right. I'll have the rest of Moncada's background waiting for you in Miami."

"Include a profile of Brandon Hall while you're at it," Carter replied. "It might help."

"Will do. And there's one more thing, N3. We think Hall gets most of his information on Tejada's personal affairs from the mistress, Lapita del Preda. You might be able to use that."

Hawk's words created a slightly bitter taste in Carter's mouth. Half this job seemed to be using people.

"I'll work on it," he said dryly. "But it would help if I

could cooperate with Hall, a brother-in-a-fellow-agency sort of thing. I'm sure he can be trusted. Are you sure I can't tell . . ."

"No way," Hawk said emphatically. "Only one other person besides Bateman and myself even knows you're alive and what you're doing. It has to stay that way."

"Right."

"Good hunting, Nick."

And good killing, Carter thought, removing the scrambler, replacing the instrument in its cradle and moving from the booth.

Carter walked across the waiting area and handed his ticket to the smiling Pan Am agent at the reservations counter.

"I've had a change in business plans. Could you please change this to the next Miami flight?"

"Certainly, sir. I'll check the schedule."

Her fingers did things to the computor console, and then she looked back up with a frown on her pretty face.

"There is a flight, sir, but . . ."

"Yes?"

"Well, I'm afraid it's a bit of a while yet."

"What's a 'bit,' my dear?"

"A three-hour wait."

Carter smiled. "That's all right. Believe me, I can use the rest."

SIX

MIAMI: FIVE WEEKS BEFORE

It was late afternoon when Carter deplaned in Miami. He cabbed to the Fontainebleau, checked in as Martin Harris-White, and deposited his bags in his room.

In minutes he had the small, black handbag loaded with the necessary hair and makeup that would turn him into Lieutenant Raul Moncada.

In the lobby he asked for messages. There weren't any, but there was a large envelope.

Back on the street, he walked some distance before hailing a cab to the Little Havana section of the city.

It took him nearly an hour of shopping to purchase a suitcase and enough cheap clothing to fill it. This done, he searched out the shop of a seamstress he had used many times before.

Helga Dornoff was an aging, tiny woman who had somehow slipped through the cracks in the mainstream of life.

She had, for years, made a living in South Miami Beach

doing alterations for local ready-to-wear shops and tending to clothing repair for tourists in the nearby beach hotels and motels.

The tinkling bell on the door of the tiny shop and living quarters brought her old gray head up from behind her sewing machine.

"Good evening, may I help you?"

"You may, *gnädige Frau*," Carter replied in his crispest German. "I have four suits and a few other assorted pieces of clothing here that require labels."

"Labels?"

"Yes, madame. I have come lately from South America, and I fear my business would suffer if German labels were seen in my clothing."

"German labels?"

"I'm sure you understand."

"Of course," the old woman said, her parched lips curving in the semblance of a smile. "I do that thing quite often for . . . Spanish-speaking people."

Carter pressed a stack of labels into her hand along with several bills. "I'm sure fifty dollars will make you drop the other work you have for the evening."

"What time will you want to pick them up?"

"It is seven now. Shall we say, ten o'clock?"

"I think I can make that."

Carter closed the door behind him with confidence. She would be substituting Brazilian labels for American labels on the clothes, but she wouldn't know the difference.

Helga Dornoff was blind.

A few blocks from the old lady's shop was the Café Castile. It was a small place, hushed and sophisticated, where serious men ate seriously and drank—just as seriously—with respect for a good wine.

He ordered a shrimp dish with a heavy Cuban sauce and kept an eye on his watch as he ate.

Carter returned to the shop a half hour early, at nine-thirty.

"I am sorry, *mein Herr*, but I am not quite finished."

"No matter. Is there a restroom?"

"In the far rear."

"*Danke.*"

Behind the locked door of the bathroom, Carter shaded out the gray from his hair and retinted it a raven black. A temporary betel dye darkened his already swarthy skin, and caps on his teeth rearranged the line of his jaw.

He removed the gray contact lenses of Harris-White. His own dark eyes would suffice for Raul Moncada. But to give the illusion of a weary, too-much-traveled man who had not slept much recently, he used some eyedrops from a special kit.

In seconds his eyes were red-rimmed and puffy.

Pictures of Lieutenant Raul Moncada were nonexistent, so Carter worked from his own imagination.

A heavy black mustache and a thickening of his brows added the final touches, then he returned to the front of the shop and the old, gray-haired woman . . .

"Is everything ready now, *gnädige Frau*?"

"*Ja*, yes, finished."

Carter paid her the exact amount she asked for, packed the clothes, and left the shop. A short stop in a public restroom, and he was wearing one of the newly labeled suits with a slightly soiled shirt and no tie.

A half hour later he was checking into a cheap hotel in downtown Miami.

"How many nights?"

"I don't know exactly," Carter replied in very broken English. "I think, maybe, three."

"That'll be thirty-eight-fifty . . . in advance."

Carter carefully counted out the bills and the exact change.

"If ya stay a fourth day ya'll hafta pay by noon or else we padlock the door."

"*Sim, sim.*"

The room was little better than the lobby, with torn bedding, cracked windowpanes, and faded wallpaper.

Carter smiled.

It was exactly the kind of place a poorly paid lieutenant in a poorly paid army would stay while on an errand of mercy to save the life of his beloved president.

Leaving the room, he cased the hall until he found what he wanted: a tiny room where the cleaning woman stored what equipment she used when she worked.

Carter guessed it was rarely.

Above the false ceiling was a perfect hiding place for Martin Harris-White's clothing in the black bag, and the briefcase.

Back in the musty room, he spent the next half hour unpacking Raul Moncada's new wardrobe and carefully arranging it in the closet. When this was done, he undressed and broke the seal on the envelope he had received at the Fontainebleau.

Then he draped himself across the lumpy bed to read himself to sleep on the background of Raul Moncada and the dossier on Brandon Hall.

Brandon Hall sat in a shadowed booth far in the rear of the Cabrillo Lounge in Little Havana. He knew the lounge and the area well. For years it had been his "beat" as an intelligence gatherer.

What were the Castro agents in the U.S. doing? What were the anti-Castro people doing? Who was buying and

selling arms? What people headed the anti-Castro revolutionary splinter groups, and who backed them?

Getting this information and passing it on to Washington had been Hall's job for five years, and he had
enjoyed it.

Then, a year ago, he had been assigned as control to the
twenty or so agents in Brazil. It started out as liaison work.
He merely collected information from the agents watching
Tejada and the forces who would overthrow Tejada, and
passed it on to Washington.

But slowly the job had changed.

Rich oil fields had been discovered in Brazil. Tejada
started making glorious plans. Brazil would soon lead the
world in oil production. Brazil would become indepen-
dent. Tejada would elevate the poor and the downtrodden.

Brandon Hall knew it was all hogwash, and he had told
State so.

"No matter," came the reply. "Tejada is anti-
Communist. He's all we have down there, so we keep him
in power."

But lately there had been new wrinkles. The guerrillas
in the hills had become more active. There were leaky
rumors from Washington, all denied, that the U.S. might
welcome a Tejada overthrow.

As a consequence, Tejada had demanded more U.S.
intelligence activity in Brazil to "watch his enemies."

Brandon Hall was in the middle. He considered Frederico Tejada an amoral despot. But his duty was to
protect the man and his regime.

And now the despot was going too far. Through a
phony Liechtenstein company, Tejada had commissioned
his own refineries to be built in Brazil. The first of a
number of supertankers would soon be carrying Brazilian
oil.

And all the profits would go to Tejada.

It stank to high heaven.

But Brandon Hall had to go along with it.

Then the order had come down: "Get more on Tejada's personal affairs . . . must know foreign business dealings . . . get proof of fraud in government."

Easy to ask, but hard to do.

But Hall had found a way. He had wormed his way into the confidence of Tejada's mistress, Lapita del Preda. Eventually he had even seduced her.

But even that had backfired. They had fallen in love.

Now Hall desperately wanted to see Tejada fall from power, if only that would release Lapita from his grip. But Hall was ordered to stand behind Tejada at every turn.

Hall sipped his beer morosely and wished he had gotten his law degree instead of deciding to be a spook.

Being a spook wasn't all it was cracked up to be.

"Senhor Hall?"

He was tall, obviously a Latin, with good features and a bearing that reminded the CIA man of the military. His clothes were cheap and not pressed too well, and the shoes on his feet needed soles and heels.

"Yes."

"My name is Moncada . . . Lieutenant Raul Moncada. I am the person who left the message at your hotel."

"What can I do for you?"

"May I sit down?"

Hall waved him into the other side of the booth. "A lieutenant in what army?"

"In the Brazilian army, *senhor*. In the army of His Excellency, President Frederico Tejada."

Hall managed to hold down the surprise in his face to a twitch in one eye.

"Are you on vacation in Miami, Lieutenant?"

"No, I am on a mission of patriotism."

"Oh?"

"I must see President Tejada."

Pinpricks of alarm ran up Hall's spine like an electric shock. In the past three years there had been five attempts on Tejada's life, two of them by men in his own cadre.

Could this lieutenant be planning a sixth, and using Hall to set it up?

"Why do you come to me?"

"Because, Senhor Hall, you can set up a meeting with my president."

Oh, God, Hall thought, but he kept his face an emotionless mask.

"Preposterous. I don't even know—"

"Senhor Hall, you are President Tejada's CIA liaison with Washington. You are in constant contact with him. Besides his own chief of intelligence, Secretary of Internal Security Carlos Panama, you are the only man he trusts. I know that Tejada is in Miami, or somewhere near Miami, and I must see him."

Hall hid his sudden chaotic feelings behind the lighting of a small cigar.

"If you must see him, Lieutenant, why don't you go through channels . . . and do it in your own country?"

Large teeth glowed in the swarthy face. "Senhor Hall, I am a lowly lieutenant. Without recommendation, my president sees no one below the rank of colonel, even in his own army."

"That's true," Hall said, biting down on the cigar a little too hard.

"And the reason for my mission—for my being in Miami—is that Tejada's enemies must not know that I have contacted him. Hence, I am here, outside my country."

Hall used time by sipping the beer and puffing on his cigar while he studied the man across the booth.

He was far from ugly, but he had the kind of face that wasn't comfortable to look at. His jaw was too large and his teeth projected oddly. The overhang of his brow so shaded his dark eyes that it was impossible to read anything in them.

"I'm afraid what you want would be impossible even if Tejada were in Miami."

"Senhor Hall, the president is, at this very moment, in a secluded, well-guarded villa near Miami Shores."

Hall shot forward until his face was only inches from the other man's. "Senhor Moncada, you are privy to information that could be very dangerous. In fact, information that could get you killed."

"I am aware of that and am prepared to take the risk. I am here to save my president's life, and . . ."

"And . . . ?"

Again the big-toothed smile. "And to insure my rise in the Brazilian military."

Hall sighed and relaxed slightly. Ambition, personal gain, advancement . . . those were things Hall could understand in the Latin way of things.

A poor boy in Latin America had only three ways to crawl out of poverty: crime, the church, or the military.

Hall took a pad and pen from his pocket and slid it across the table. "Write down your serial number, your mother's and father's first names, your place of birth, and your current duty station."

"I cannot give you my current duty station."

"Why not?"

"Because if it is checked, it would jeopardize my current mission on the president's behalf."

Hall half believed him for some odd reason. "All right. Give me the rest of the information."

Carter did as he was asked and slid the pad back toward the other man.

"I'll be right back."

Carter appropriated the remainder of Hall's beer and lit a cigarette.

The CIA man would be calling the villa. Within seconds, Tejada's chief of intelligence, Carlos Panama, would be on the phone to Brasília.

They would find out that Lieutenant Raul Moncada existed, but that was about all.

It was twenty minutes before Hall returned.

"All right, Lieutenant, what proof do you have that President Tejada is in danger or that there is some sort of coup in the planning?"

"That information, *senhor*, is for Tejada's ears only," Carter said quietly.

Hall seemed to hesitate, but Carter knew that the next step had already been formulated in the man's mind.

"All right. Where are you staying in Miami?"

Carter gave him the address and room number of the hotel. He could see the man doing some quick calculating.

"Go back to your hotel. I will contact you by eight o'clock tonight."

Carter nodded and stood. "You will not be sorry you are doing this, Senhor Hall. I guarantee it."

He walked from the lounge at a brisk, military pace and killed almost an hour meandering the streets before taking a public bus back to the hotel.

They had done a good job of searching the room. Hardly anything was disturbed. But while they were trained to be good, a Killmaster was trained to be an expert.

He easily spotted what had been disturbed by their searching fingers.

Hall's men had found just enough to prove that Raul

Moncada appeared to be exactly who he said he was.

Carter checked the hall, then made his way down to the storage room where the maid kept her cleaning equipment. He mounted a short stepladder, pushed up one square of the false, composition board ceiling, and retrieved the leather briefcase. He left the black bag. If all went well, it would be retrieved later.

Back in his room he showered, shaved, and then spread the betel nut makeup all over his body. This done, he dressed and stretched across the bed.

They came at ten o'clock.

The quick rap on the door awakened him instantly. Without hurrying, he tugged on a suit jacket, picked up the briefcase, and opened the door.

Hall wasn't there, but the three rugged-looking men who were had ''government'' stamped all over them. One of them eyed the briefcase with a frown.

''Raul Moncada?''

''Yes, I'm ready.''

''You know who we are?''

Carter smiled. ''Gentlemen, I've seen your brothers running all over my country since I was a boy. Shall we go? I am very eager to meet with my president.''

Carter lit the last cigarette in his pack and checked his watch; it was one o'clock in the morning.

He had given Frederico Tejada an identical copy of the plan he had given General Pablo Fernandes in Paris. It was now two hours later.

Would Tejada, Hall, and the wily little intelligence chief buy it?

There had been barely ten words said between Carter and the others after he had handed over the plan.

Now he waited in a kitchen alcove in front of a cold cup of coffee, with two of Carlos Panama's steel-eyed henchmen watching over him.

"More coffee, Lieutenant?"

"*Não*," Carter replied, shaking his head and plastering a look of worry on his face.

Both of Panama's agents had subtly grilled him during the past two hours.

They were good, both of them. But then they should have been. They were trained by the master himself, Carlos Panama.

Carter had managed to answer eighty percent of the questions with reasonable replies that would be almost impossible to check. The other twenty percent he had merely parried.

"Could I have another cigarette?"

"Certainly."

The man was halfway across the room toward Carter, the pack extended, when the door opened and a third bodyguard filled the opening.

"They want him."

Carter stood and followed them through the rambling villa to Tejada's private suite.

The big man himself was little, barely five-feet-eight, with narrow, stooped shoulders and spindly legs. He was about fifty, but his dark, masklike face was ageless and seemed to register nothing but a constant scowl.

Tejada was in pajamas and a conservative dark blue robe. He sat like a ramrod-stiff Napoleon behind a small desk at the foot of the bed. Hall stood to his right, and Carlos Panama lounged in a large chair to Tejada's left, in the shadows.

Carter knew that it was Panama he would have to

convince more than the others. For that reason, he took a stance slightly to the left of the desk when he entered the room.

"Lieutenant Moncada . . ."

"*Sim, meu Presidente.*"

"We have read this document several times." Tejada looked up from the desk with the most withering stare he could muster. Carter simulated tension, nervousness, and fear. "First of all, how did this happen to come into your possession?"

"A month ago I was contacted by a colonel . . ."

"What colonel?" Panama asked from his cocoon of darkness.

"I don't know his name."

"Go on," Tejada urged.

"He said that he was on the personal staff of General Fernandes. He appealed to me as a patriot and as a product of the poor in our country. He said, *meu Presidente*—and forgive me, for these are his words—that you plan on raping Brazil."

"A pig, Fernandes!" Tejada declared, slamming his fist on the table.

"Continue, Lieutenant," Panama hissed.

"He said it was time we had a new government, one that would be more responsive to the people. I smelled a coup right then and decided to go along with the man until I could learn more."

"Yes, yes," Tejada cried, waving the papers, "but this plan!"

"I received it one week ago. I was told that over forty junior officers in Rio, Brasília, and in the smaller provinces had agreed to the coup."

"But you were told none of their names?" Hall asked.

"No. I was told to study the plan and then to destroy it."

"And then . . . ?"

"And then," Carter replied, "I was told to wait. The exact date and time of the plan's execution would be given to me twenty-four hours before."

Tejada stood, walked around the desk, and embraced him. "Lieutenant, this patriotism will not be ignored. I thank you, and your country thanks you!"

"It is merely my duty, Your Excellency."

Carlos Panama's lean and hungry face appeared at Tejada's shoulder. He had one good eye and one glass eye. They both seemed to bore into Carter's brain and soul.

"We will arrange for your quiet return to Brazil, Lieutenant. Through my people, a system of communications will be set up so that you can warn us the moment word comes down that the coup is on."

"Senhor Panama . . . Your Excellency," Carter said, forcing a quiver of humbleness into his voice, "if I may be so bold . . ."

"Yes?"

"I have an alternate plan that I have done a great deal of work on. If I could only suggest . . ."

The three men exchanged glances. Finally, Panama shrugged. "It will do no harm to listen."

"Sit down, Lieutenant," Tejada said. "I will ring for some brandy."

It took Carter nearly an hour to recite, in the minutest detail, the counterplan the talented boys at AXE had worked out for a mock operation in a mock country. It was very easy for Carter to substitute real people and places for their fictitious one.

Halfway through the recitation, all three men were nodding in mutual agreement.

When Carter sat back in silence at last, President Tejada was beaming. Carlos Panama was smiling as much as he ever smiled, and Brandon Hall was openly scowling.

"It has few flaws," Panama offered.

"It has the planning of a general, not a lieutenant," Tejada sighed.

"I don't like it," Hall said. "If it all came down this way, my people will be right in the thick of it."

"You should be!" Tejada roared. "If you had been in the thick of it already, it would have been *your* people who would have discovered this threat to my government instead of one of my own officers!"

Carter could feel the sudden tension among the three men, and he knew he had to defuse it. It was imperative that the CIA be on the scene not as combatants, but as observers to file the proper reports to Washington.

"Senhor Hall, you and your people will only be a backup. I have no objections to you taking the credit for this discovery. I would think your State Department would welcome the firsthand information you will be able to give them, that a coup has been stopped and all is quiet and safe with my president's government."

Hall winced. He knew he was beaten, and Carter knew that the CIA man would have to go along with the plan if Tejada and Panama approved it.

A half hour later, they did.

"I will arrange your transportation back to Rio, Lieutenant," Panama said, rising.

"No, please. I smuggled myself out of the country; I think it would be much better if I got back in the same way. I don't think agents of General Fernandes are watching me, but one never knows."

Panama exchanged a quick look with Tejada, and both men nodded.

"Fine. We will return you to downtown Miami, and you can make your own way back to your hotel. Here is my private number at Government House."

"Good," Carter said and stood. "I will contact you in Rio within a week's time."

As Carter was ushered from the room, he glanced one last time at Brandon Hall.

The man's scowl had deepened perceptibly.

Carter stayed in the hotel room only long enough to pack all of Moncada's belongings.

Back on the street, he walked the four blocks to the bus station and bought a ticket to Key West.

Hall's men were over him like a blanket. They were good, almost always out of sight, but there.

Carter slept the entire trip and felt fairly refreshed when the bus pulled into the seaside resort at nine o'clock that morning.

The CIA boys were still there, in two cars, and they looked far from refreshed after the long drive.

He checked into a cheap hotel near the bus station and immediately headed for the beach. In a tiny café he ate a leisurely breakfast and eyeballed the various sport fishing boats bobbing along the piers.

By the time the meal was over and he had finished two cigarettes over coffee, he had chosen the boat.

"Rafe Christopher. Yeah, the *Sea Dog*'s my boat. You don't look like no fisherman."

"I am not, sir. I am just a lover of the sea. I would like to rent your boat for the day just to sail the Keys and sense the sea around me."

The look on the man's bearded and weathered face read

"bullshit," but he readily agreed when Carter didn't balk at his price.

"Eight o'clock? You mean you wanna take a *night* cruise?"

"Yes."

"That'll be another ten bucks an hour."

Again Carter readily agreed.

He wasted the afternoon in bars and idly browsing in the many souvenir stands that lined the tiny streets leading inward from the beach.

At six o'clock he ate again and returned to his hotel. He carefully wiped the room and the suitcase clean of all fingerprints, and then he napped until a quarter of eight.

At eight sharp he stepped aboard the *Sea Dog* with only the small black bag containing the identity of Martin Harris-White in his hand.

"You got any direction or place in particular you'd like to go, mister?"

"Yes, as a matter of fact, I do. Do you know Long Key?"

"Like the back of my hand."

"Good. I'd like to go there . . . on the Gulf side."

"Ten minutes," the old seaman said and disappeared below.

Carter took a deck chair and guessed it would be two minutes before the man found a reason to hit the beach.

He was right on the nose.

"Damn," Rafe Christopher exclaimed, his cap and beard emerging first from the hatch.

"What is it?"

"Beer. There's no beer in the cooler. If we're gonna motor around the Gulf half the night, I'd like a little taste now and then. You mind?"

Carter shrugged and watched the old seaman's rolling

gait until he was out of sight.

Rafe Christopher, Carter thought, dragging deeply on his cigarette, was a terrible actor.

When Carter made the lights of Marathon, on Voca Key, he unholstered Wilhelmina and, holding the Luger low by his leg, walked into the wheelhouse.

"That's Voca Key over there," Christopher said. "We're about ten miles from Long Key."

"I know," Carter said. "How much did they give you, Rafe Christopher?"

"Huh?"

"The three men you talked to while you bought the beer."

"I don't know what the hell you're . . ."

Carter brought the Luger up until its blue steel glowed in the dim dashlights.

"How much, Rafe?"

"Nothin', man, I swear! Listen, they're government men, showed me their IDs. I don't know what you've done, but I don't want no trouble."

"And you won't get any, Rafe, if you do what I tell you. Do you know Shark Point?"

"On the mainland?"

"That's right."

"Yeah, I know it. But those guys'll be waitin' for you—"

"On Long Key, out here. But we're going to Shark Point . . . up there. Bring her around."

"My bill, please."

"Of course, Mr. Harris-White. Was everything satisfactory?"

"Extremely. My Barbados tickets?"

"Yes, sir. They made them up the moment you called."

In the airport bus, Carter consulted an airline timetable.

There was an Air Brazil flight from Barbados to Rio the following afternoon at three o'clock.

Excellent, he thought; he would get some sun this afternoon and a good night's sleep.

Idly, his eye caught the date on a newspaper in another passenger's hands.

Just four weeks to go.

SEVEN

RIO: NOW

After leaving the Swede, Carter had returned to the Avenida Rio Branco and played tourist until he was sure that no one was following him.

Now he waited patiently in the long post office line. It had been nearly an hour since he had left Lindeman, and all of it had been spent walking. His skin, beneath the double layer of clothing, was oozing perspiration in buckets, and he had to constantly mop his face.

Much more of this, he thought, *and Salvatore Bellini's complexion will have to be radically repaired.*

"*Senhor?*"

"*Sim.* A package from Paris. My name is Bellini . . . Salvatore Bellini."

Carefully, Carter laid his passport and the shipping stub from the Paris post office on the counter.

"One moment."

It was several before the man returned with the oblong package.

"Sign right there, *senhor*."

Carter signed with a flourish and moved back into the sunlight.

It was four blocks to the public baths. There he would secrete the contents of the package in Salvatore Bellini's false fat.

"Will that be all, Your Excellency?"

"Yes, yes, yes."

President Frederico Tejada waved a hand at his aide, then adjusted the bemedaled and beribboned tunic across his chest.

The aide slid quietly backward through the door and closed it just as quietly behind him as Tejada ran a gentle sleeve over the gleaming medals. The blazing noontime sun coming from the huge vaulted bay windows danced from their surfaces and brought a smile to his face.

Most of the ribbons and medals had been awarded to Tejada by Tejada during his eight-year reign. He called it "rule" or "reign" only to himself and the people closest to him, of course. To the masses, the populace, it was his presidency through two terms of office. Tejada still called them "terms of office" even though he had abolished general elections the day his coup had catapulted him into power.

He lit a cigarette and moved to the window. He savored the first smoke of the day as he savored the day itself. This would be his crowning day. In eight years he had brought his country back to the far right, back under the wing of the United States.

True, they were sometimes unhappy with his extreme policies of repression, but he had stifled the opposition party by bringing their leader, Luís Braz, into his cabinet and by managing to squelch the rebels in the hills. They

still existed, of course, but without the backing of Braz
and his party, they had no power.

Their drastic failure during the last of four coup attempts a year before had proved that.

Braz was getting too popular and too powerful again,
but any hope of influence he might have would end with
this day's celebration. With United States money, Tejada
had tapped new oil fields in his country. The engineers
had said they could well be the biggest energy find of the
century.

And today the *Tejada*, the newest supertanker in the
world, would sail into Guanabara Bay with his first ship-
ment north. He, *O Presidente*—cheered on by the multitudes that loved him—would board that tanker for the
christening ceremonies and send it on its way.

It would be the first of a whole fleet of tankers and the
first of billions of gallons of oil that would produce dollars
for his country . . . and his private accounts in Liechtenstein.

Only Tejada knew of those accounts. That was why he
was still president. He trusted no one with his personal
affairs.

"Your Excellency?"

"Yes . . . yes?"

"The report you asked for . . ."

Tejada took the folder and again dismissed the aide with
a wave of his hand. He turned back to the windows' light
and opened the dossier. Quickly he scanned the two
pages, then snorted in disgust.

"Intelligence I have in abundance throughout the
cities. In the provinces, they can't even locate the complete record of a lowly lieutenant!"

He made a mental note to correct that as soon as possible. A third of his state police and army were in little

hamlets and villages that often were forgotten.

The lieutenant in question, Raul Moncada, was probably from those ranks. Tejada hoped so. A great deal depended on the man's information and his use as a liaison with the CIA people.

"Nothing, absolutely *nothing*, must ruin this perfect day!" he hissed, slapping the folder down on a small table by his right hand. "Not even another stupid coup attempt!"

Not that it wasn't a brilliant plan; it was a daring plan conceived by an equally daring man. General Pablo Fernandes was certainly capable of both brilliance and bravado. If he weren't, Tejada would never have elevated him so high—high enough to want it all in the form of the presidency itself.

And the Russians . . . stupid dolts to back Fernandes!

Tejada didn't know this for sure, however. He had only the word of Raul Moncada, the young lieutenant. And that same lieutenant's assurance of loyalty and the ability to stop the coup he had stumbled across.

But the idiots in the outlying regions of his country, far from the capital, couldn't come up with a complete dossier on Lieutenant Raul Moncada.

Tejada's eyes traveled to the folder. They misted, and the image of Moncada's dark face and tall, lean body took form.

He could still see the man that day a month before as he had stood before Tejada, quaking, outlining Fernandes's plot for a coup.

Tejada had listened as the lieutenant offered to enter the plot and forward all information concerning troop strength, traitors, and areas to be attacked to the American CIA observers and men close to the president.

Tejada had hesitated, as had Carlos Panama. But almost daily since their return from Miami, Moncada had been in touch with information that was damning to Fernandes. He had passed along definitive proof of Russian arms shipments to General Fernandes and even more lurid details of the plan of attack.

But in all this time—nearly a month—Panama had not been able to come up with a complete background on Moncada. The man's background was as much a mystery as he was now a phantom.

He had stayed in hiding all this time, and appeared at the damnedest times and in the damnedest places.

But each time, his information had been accurate and his loyalty unquestionable.

Tejada let smoke drift from his nostrils and moved his eyes upward over the nearby mountains to the blue-domed sky and to the sun that was also shining over central Brazil.

At that moment his own crack paramilitary commandos, under the guidance of CIA logistics, would be positioned around Brasília to quash the coup and capture Fernandes.

But Tejada would not have Fernandes executed.

No, he would show his people and the world the mercy of his nature and the democracy of his government. He would try the general, have him imprisoned for a short time, and then exiled.

An assassin would be hired later to kill him in a foreign country.

"Your Excellency?"

"*Sim?*"

"Your car is ready."

The president nodded. He checked his tunic again, set the braided hat on his steel-gray hair, tilted it at a rakish angle, then turned to his aide.

"I am ready." He glanced at the huge wall clock over the door and smiled.

In four hours he would consolidate his reign for another four years.

His mind was filled with thoughts of the future as he followed his aide from the room.

At no time had the thought entered Frederico Tejada's mind that in four hours he would be dead.

Twelve hundred miles inland from Rio, the noon sun glinted on the dark steel skin of a helicopter as it lofted above the Praça dos Três Poderes on the outskirts of Brasília.

In it, his eyes red-rimmed from lack of sleep and his green battle fatigues wrinkled and rank from three days' wear, sat General Pablo Fernandes.

From his aerial vantage point he would soon be able to watch every aspect of his bid for power.

It had been a long, and sometimes degrading, road for Fernandes. Unlike Tejada, he was no heir to political power, nor was his background part of the upper class. He had come from peasant stock, from the coffee farmers in the state of Bahia.

But he had educated himself. He had learned to read and write, and he had learned to watch and listen. From those in power, he learned deceit and treachery. He had learned, and he had become a master. Step by step, his career had blossomed under one dictator after another.

Fernandes had always been able to smell out the winds of change. He made sure that he was included in each new bid for power. He guaranteed himself another rung up the ladder of military rank with each coup.

Now he was the general of generals, and there was only one remaining step.

The fact that the Americans considered him incapable of ruling, and the Russians required his assurance of their participation in his government before they would give him their aid, meant little.

He would dictate to the Americans because of the oil and, in turn, use them to break his ties with Moscow. And with both superpowers in check, Fernandes would rule at his pleasure.

There would be one man, one rule, and one coffer into which would pour the dollars, the pounds, the francs, the marks, and all the other currency generated by his oil.

Even as he looked down on the gleaming capital, his gaze fell naturally to the Palácio da Alvorada, the splendid home of the president, rather than the Palácio do Planalto, the offices where the president toiled.

Fernandes planned on very little toil. The sheiks didn't toil. And Fernandes, when he came to power, planned on being a Latin American sheik.

It had long been his dream, but the plan and the opportunity had never come up.

Then the tall, blond Swede had approached him in Paris. He had just materialized in Fernandes's hotel room one evening, right through the security of his bodyguards.

The Swede's plan was brilliant, a stroke of military genius. And the coup de grace was equal to it.

The destruction of the tanker in Rio, with Tejada aboard, would cause instant chaos. And the simultaneous capture of Brasília would lay the remnants of Tejada's government in his, Fernandes's hands.

The Swede's price was high: an agreement with Fernandes that he would keep his oil prices in line with the OPEC nations. That, to Fernandes, was better than the man's first demand that he join OPEC. For Fernandes, that was impossible. It was to be *his* oil and *his* country.

He would align with no one. The Swede had finally accepted the latter agreement.

What did Fernandes care? He would tell them all to go to hell once the oil was his.

He wondered who manipulated the Swede. Was it the Russians? OPEC? Some even more private interests?

It was probably the Russians. It was their style.

It mattered little to Fernandes. The man would never report back to his superiors anyway. And he deserved to die. One search of his room had easily turned up his passport. Without his passport, Bijorn Lindeman could not leave the country.

At that moment, Fernandes's handpicked men were moving in to cluster at every exit point from Rio. Their orders were simple: intercept the Swede, Bijorn Lindeman, and execute immediately.

"General!"

"*Sim?*" He turned to his aide and pilot.

"Please . . . English," said the Russian in the jump seat behind him.

The general smiled. *Insolent pig. But just wait!*

"English," he said to the pilot.

"The first and second divisions are in place."

Fernandes checked his watch.

Four hours.

"Soon," his voice rasped. "Very soon."

EIGHT

RIO: FOUR WEEKS BEFORE

The elevator, old, with a folding gate instead of a door, deposited him in the basement of the Ministry Building with a clank. He shivered slightly when he stepped into the hall and walked with a tired step toward the only marked door at its far end.

Bold block letters on the frosted glass announced himself to himself: Luís Braz.

Beneath the name, in letters so small they could hardly be read, was the title of his office: Minister of Internal Commerce.

Luís Braz smiled.

In days gone by, there could have been several titles under his name: Minister of Revolution, Guerrilla Fighter, Intellectual of the Masses, Realist.

But no more.

Luís Braz had been all of those things and had retired from them.

Now he was minister of a nonexistent domestic commerce, and he wished he were back in Portugal, in exile.

His last office, in Lisbon, as the head of the revolutionary government in exile, had been more spacious than this.

And a damned sight warmer, he mused.

He pushed the door. It stuck. He shoved an ample hip against it. It flew open and bounced against the desk. The outer cubicle, his secretary's "office," had barely enough space for her desk, a file cabinet, a chair, and a plant.

The plant was dying.

She was shuffling papers on top of the cabinet. "One day that glass will break," she said.

"Can't they shave the door?" He slammed it shut.

"I've asked . . . ten times. You didn't wear your sweater."

"I forgot. Ask them again, before I break the glass!"

"I will, but it won't do any good."

She sidestepped the six inches to her chair and sat. Without looking up, she studied the pad in front of her and, at the same time, bawled him out for inviting pneumonia and sixteen other assorted viruses into his valuable body.

Luís Braz paid no attention and looked adoringly at the top of her dark head. Slowly, a smile crept over his wrinkled and aging features.

She was his housekeeper, his confidante, his cook, his secretary, his conscience, and . . . his daughter.

"Now, your appointments—"

He interrupted. "You sound like your mother."

She looked up. The smile was full of even, white teeth in a very sweet face that still managed to look sultry. "Do I? Good!"

"At twenty-five you should be married and putting that sexy figure to good use."

"You shouldn't talk to your daughter like that."

"I know, but the truth just seems to bubble out of me now and then."

"Did you remember your pills?"

He patted his pocket. It was empty.

"Yes," he lied.

"You have four appointments today. Alex is waiting in your office with the reports, and Carlos Panama has already called three times."

"Why? Does he want to put me back in jail?"

An obvious shiver went through her body, but Leonora Braz managed a smile and a flip answer.

"I think he and Tejada would like to, but they know that would only bring the young ones out of the hills and start the revolution over again."

"And you, my daughter, what would you do if the young ones—my old students—came down from the hills with their guns?"

"Find me a gun," she said without batting an eye.

Luís Braz nodded and took four steps toward the door of his office. "What's for dinner tonight?"

"Something that will agree with your diet."

He made a disgusted sound and moved through the door, not bothering to close it behind him.

Alexander Dragos vaulted to his feet with a brisk "Good morning" and a lengthy inquiry into the state of Luís Braz's health.

"I'm dying, you fool," Braz said. "I've been doing it for years and I see no reason to stop now. Coffee!" He moved around the desk and settled into a high-backed leather chair, his only carryover from his years of exile.

Dragos jumped. He hated the bitter, strong coffee that Braz started each day with, but, as he had done for years, he poured two cups.

"The latest inflation reports and the memorandums from the bankers are on your desk."

"What do they say?"

"The inflation reports are lies, and the bankers want you to do something about it."

"What, for instance?"

"Talk to Tejada and convince him that we don't need supertankers for the oil. Show him that the country is going to hell in a hand basket."

"Coffee," Braz growled, sweeping the papers into a wastebasket with one hand and reaching for the phone with the other.

By the time he got through to Carlos Panama, Dragos had placed a cup of inky, strong-smelling coffee by his arm.

"Luís Braz, Mr. Secretary, returning your calls."

"Ah yes, Braz. I want you to investigate your tax folios on the name Moncada."

Braz glowered at the phone. "All of them, Mr. Secretary?"

"Of course all of them!"

"There must be hundreds of Moncadas, Mr. Secretary."

"I know that, damnit! Just do it! And narrow them down to head-of-household or sons named Raul."

"Yes, Mr. Secretary. We will get right on it."

Luís Braz wished his office could accomplish something besides tracking down people so Carlos Panama's secret police could put them in jail.

"One other thing, Braz. Your Communist comrades

in the mountains have started their nuisance raids again . . ."

The back of Luís Braz's neck burned red. "They are not Communists, Mr. Secretary."

"Yes, yes, I know that's what you say, but it's no matter. I want it stopped. That's why you are part of the government, so you can keep those hoodlums in check."

"If I can't contact—"

"You can, Luís, and I know it. You are in constant contact with Ortez and the others, and I know it. Stop them, Luís, or people in the provinces will start disappearing again."

"Bastard snake," Braz muttered under his breath.

"What's that?"

"I will do what I can, Mr. Secretary."

"See that you do."

The voice was replaced by a dial tone, and Braz recradled the instrument.

"Dragos . . ."

"Yes, sir?"

"Contact Ortez. Tell him to stop these stupid raids. He's only going to get himself and a lot of innocent people slaughtered."

Dragos's jaw clamped shut until the line along the edge of it went white.

"These are the times I wish I hadn't heeded your summons . . . the times I wish I had stayed in the hills."

Luís Braz's face fell, and his tone when he spoke again softened. "I know, old friend, but our revolution is over. It's best now to survive."

"I know . . . damnit. I'll get an order off to him this afternoon."

"Request, Alex, a *request*. We don't issue orders. We

are no longer an army.''

"Yes, sir.''

"And pick that crap out of the wastebasket and file it. What time is it?''

"Two minutes to twelve, sir,'' Dragos replied with a smile as his boss stood and ambled toward the door.

"I'm going to lunch.''

"I know, sir.''

Luís Braz went to lunch every day at exactly twelve o'clock. By going at noon, he didn't have to meet and talk to the other ministers who all ate at one o'clock in the officials' dining room.

Carter entered the great, mausoleumlike lobby of the Ministry Building and made his way toward the wide bank of receptionists in its center.

"Good morning, my dear,'' Carter said, laying his credentials in front of a youngish, pretty girl with darting eyes that photographed him like a camera.

"*Senhor?*''

"I am Martin Harris-White, with the BBC in Latin America. I have an appointment with Senhor Eulio Paramaine.''

"And your business, *senhor*?''

Carter's eyes didn't move from hers, but he saw her right hand flick the switch that would record his every word. Tomorrow morning, that recording—along with a hundred others—would be fed onto a master tape in the offices of Carlos Panama.

"I am negotiating to do a documentary on this year's carnival. I've been given to understand that Senhor Paramaine's permission must be obtained in the matter.''

"*Sim, senhor*. One moment.''

Using the telephone and speaking very quietly, she checked with someone above.

"The fourth floor, *senhor*. Here is your pass. It will be checked by a guard on each floor."

"Really?"

"*Sim, senhor*. The revolutionary terrorists are everywhere. All the officials here in the Ministry Building must be protected."

"Yes, I am sure they must. The elevators . . . there?"

"I am sorry, but the public elevators are not running. You will have to walk up."

Carter headed for the stairs, allowing a slight smile to play around his lips.

Yes, Carter thought, all the government officials would be protected—except one; Luís Braz would be watched, yes, but not protected.

Luís Braz had nothing to fear from the terrorists, and Carlos Panama knew it.

Carter climbed to the fourth floor, passing lazy-eyed guards who waved him along with barely a glance at his pass.

The fourth-floor guard was especially peeved when he was distracted from the magazine he was reading.

"Last door on the right," he mumbled.

Paramaine was the Minister of Culture. His outer office was even more full than Carter had expected. Even though he had an appointment, he was given a number.

Senhor Paramaine expected everyone to wait in line to pay him his bribe.

Carter waited fifteen minutes, then approached the secretary's desk.

"I say, could you direct me to the loo?"

"The loo, *senhor* . . . ?"

"Cavalheiros."

"Oh, yes. Across the hall, next to the officials' elevator."

Carter checked his watch as he crossed the hall. It was exactly 11:50.

The dial above the elevator door told him the car was on the third floor.

In the restroom, he quickly removed a pair of blue coveralls and leather gloves from his briefcase, and put them on.

Seconds later, he was through the false ceiling and moving along the catwalk toward the elevator's emergency escape door. Its hinges had not been checked for years, so it took all his strength to force it aside. Once this was done, he was sliding down the cables to the top of the elevator car itself.

With the aid of a penlight and a screwdriver, he opened the power control box and quickly traced the circuitry. He had just finished attaching two alligator clips to the relay wires, and was readying the second two that would short the circuit, when the car began to descend.

He counted. "Two . . . one . . . main lobby."

It was 11:57.

The car jolted and bumped back upward to three. The gate opened and then barely closed before the old elevator started down again.

"Two . . . one . . . lobby . . . basement."

Carter smiled.

It was noon sharp.

When the car started back up, Carter attached the second two alligator clips and reached for the handle on the trapdoor.

Luís Braz listened to the rusted cables groan, and he

wondered if this would be the day that they would give way and send him plummeting to his death in the sub-basement.

What a fitting end, he thought, to the tired old man who had one day dreamed of leading his country toward a true democracy without internal corruption and the pressures of external rule.

At last the elevator stopped, and he was able to muscle the steel gate open.

It took several seconds for the power to engage, and as it did, Luís Braz lit his one cigar of the day.

Halfway between the basement and the lobby, the car jerked to a halt, nearly throwing him to the floor. As he scrambled for the cigar that had fallen from his fingers, the trapdoor opened and a tall, rangy man in blue coveralls dropped to the floor beside him.

It was not unusual for the elevator to malfunction, but it *was* unusual for a repairman to arrive in less than an hour.

"Luís Braz?" the man said, calmly offering him a fresh light for his cigar from a gold lighter.

"*Sim.*"

"Shall we sit down? I have a great deal to explain and very little time to do it in."

"Who the devil . . . ?"

"If you must have a name, Senhor Braz, it is Martin Harris-White. But I assure you it means nothing. I have many names."

"You're from Tejada . . . or Carlos Panama."

"Quite the opposite, I assure you."

"Then who the devil are you?"

"I am, Luís Braz, the man who is going to make you president of Brazil."

NINE

RIO: NOW

The sun was nearing its zenith in a clear blue sky. The temperature was warm but not uncomfortable for Frederico Tejada, even in his starched uniform as he sat in the back of his limousine. He smiled and waved as the procession of guard cars ahead of and behind the limousine wound its way down the Avenida Presidente Vargas toward the bay.

Suddenly, from the shoreline, a cheer erupted, so loud that even the air-conditioned, insulated interior silence of the car was shattered.

Tejada leaned forward and, through the bulletproof glass, saw the reason for it. At that moment, circling around the point of Santos Dumont Airport, appeared the mammoth hull of the *Tejada*.

Awe mixed with glee on the president's face as more and more of the giant tanker crawled into view like a huge prehistoric monster. It moved through the water, even with its bulk, with the grace of a giant cat.

The telephone in the console at his side buzzed. The buzz denoted the direct line. The red line.

"Sim?"

"Meu Presidente?"

"Sim?"

Tejada recognized the voice instantly. It was Moncada—Lieutenant Raul Moncada who, in many ways, was responsible for this moment, this day.

"All is quiet but in readiness. Even now I can see the troops of Fernandes moving toward the capital. Our American friends have positioned themselves accordingly. There will be no error."

"You are there, Lieutenant? You are sure?"

"At this moment I am on the roof of the Palácio da Alvorada in Brasília with Senhor Hall, the American. It will be over in less than an hour."

"I want him alive, Lieutenant. I want all his followers annihilated, but I want Fernandes alive!"

"It will be as you wish, Your Excellency. Your air force awaits my signal; your ground troops await Senhor Hall's command. There will be nothing today for you, *meu Presidente*, but glory."

"Moncada, you will be a general in a year's time. You have my word on it."

"I would be lying, *meu Presidente*, if I did not admit that I seek such a reward."

"And you shall have it."

President Frederico Tejada replaced the phone and settled back in the car's cushiony leather with a very audible sigh.

"Good news, *meu Presidente*?"

"Excellent . . . excellent news, Luís."

Tejada rolled his head to the side and stared at Luís Braz, his Minister of Internal Commerce.

Odd, he thought, so very odd. It would seem that Braz and not Fernandes would attempt this coup. But then, that was why he had brought Braz, the leader of the opposition party, into his cabinet. To create an ally out of an enemy.

"I am glad, *meu Presidente*."

"Where is Carlos? He should be with us now."

"He is checking security at the docks. He told me he would join you on the yacht."

Tejada sighed again and accepted the drink Luís Braz had poured for him from the limousine's bar.

It was a good day.

Its only sour note was Lapita, his mistress. The note, handed to him by an aide as he had descended from his quarters, had been a shock but one he would get over.

Women! Dear God, how foolish they are!

She had fallen in love and had flown to Paris to meet her lover.

What in God's name could her lover—no matter who he was—give her that he, Frederico Tejada, could not?

Ah well, there would soon be other mistresses, and younger ones.

From this day hence, Frederico Tejada would have many mistresses—young and nubile mistresses.

"Luís?"

"*Sim*?"

"The time."

"One o'clock, *meu Presidente*. You will board the tanker in three hours."

"It will be a great day, Luís, a great day for us all."

"*Sim, meu Presidente*," Luís Braz replied, not looking at the bemedaled man sitting beside him.

There was more conversation from the other seat, but Braz did not hear it. His mind was filled with other thoughts.

It was astounding, almost unreal, after the years of struggle, the defeats, the final capitulation. But it was about to happen.

In three hours, he—Luís Braz—would be president of Brazil.

Carter replaced the phone and stepped from the booth. Gently he touched the wrinkles on his face. They were growing loose. Most of them had already disappeared from his hands. Beneath the double layer of clothing, he could feel perspiration drenching his skin.

It didn't matter. Soon Bellini would disappear, and his skin would breathe better clothed only in the dark blue summer suit of Martin Harris-White.

He checked his watch: three hours.

It would take about an hour once he was on Sugar Loaf to set everything up.

That meant he had plenty of time, more than enough, to kill Carlos Panama.

TEN

RIO: THREE WEEKS BEFORE

Police sirens screamed through the Rio night on Avenida Atlântica past posh Copacabana Beach. Carter paid them no attention as he strolled through the milling crowd of young people.

They were out for the night, as they always were in Rio. They moved in groups of six or ten, from one disco to another.

The beach itself was a city within a city. It stretched for three and a half miles, with the ocean and a ribbon of pure white sand on one side, and tall skyscrapers on the other.

The outdoor cafés, the huge hotels, and everywhere the sound of laughter and music, gave Copacabana an atmosphere all its own.

But Carter cared little for the atmosphere. He was looking for a woman in a lightweight black trench coat, black stockings, and a black silk scarf knotted around her neck.

And then he saw her just as she saw him. There was a single look and then a nod of recognition.

She had been standing beneath a garish neon sign proclaiming *Dancing All Night*. When she turned and strolled quickly away, Carter fell into place about fifty yards behind her.

At the end of three blocks she turned inland, away from the sea. Carter also turned, and found a narrow, barely lit street that angled steeply up a hill.

Around the first bend she awaited him, partially hidden in the shadows of a doorway.

"Harris-White?"

"Yes," Carter replied, joining her. "Leonora Braz?"

"Yes," she whispered, her eyes darting from him to the street. "As usual, there are bodyguards in the front and rear of the house . . ."

"Bodyguards," Carter said with a grin, "or body watchers?"

She smiled, and her face glowed in a single shaft of illumination from a distant streetlight.

She had a nice smile and a beautiful face. Her black hair was pulled back severely and twisted into a chignon at the nape of her neck.

"Your servants are off?"

"Yes. My father insisted that they had been working too hard. He hates to deceive them. Most of them are loyal. But we know that one among them is an informer for Carlos Panama."

"But we can enter the house through their quarters without Panama's men seeing us?"

"Yes, this way."

Carter moved on up the hill a half step behind her shoulder. The farther they went, the less light penetrated from the beach area behind them, until the street was almost totally black.

Now Carter knew why Braz had insisted that he use

Leonora as a guide all the way from the Avenida Atlântica. He would have never found his way without her.

"This way, down this alley. It leads to the house
alongside ours. How nimble are you?"

"Very."

"Good. You will have to jump a full story out a window. We are almost there."

Somehow in the blackness she found a door Carter
could not even see. It opened with a creaking sound and
closed the same way behind them.

"Have you the light?"

Carter pulled a penlight from his pocket and snapped it
on.

They were in an entryway. Beside them was an empty
garage stall, and directly in front of them was a narrow
wooden stairway. Halfway up, Carter saw a landing
whose balustrade was formed by a single wooden rail
resting on wooden uprights.

"The stairway goes to the roof. We will stop at the
landing. Watch your step; some of the boards are rotted."

At the landing, they stopped. To their right, above the
stall, was a window. It was open.

"Did you get out this way?"

"Yes. There is a drain. It will support my weight but
not yours. Come along."

Carter walked carefully behind her, and then he helped
her through the window.

"Give me the light!"

He did, then heard, more than saw, her shimmying
down the pipe.

Seconds later the light, shielded by her hands, came on,
illuminating a patch of ground twenty feet below.

"Jump!" she whispered.

Carter was sweating as he eased through the small

window. At last he was sitting on the ledge, his legs dangling in the air.

"Jump!" she hissed again.

Lady, Carter thought, *I can't see a damned thing*.

But he jumped, landed with a jolt, and came upright intact.

"Not pretty," she said with a chuckle, "but adequate."

"Thanks very much," he said and cased the area.

They were in a small garden. Jacaranda trees lined its border, and beneath them lilies and orchids grew like wildflowers.

They were barely across it and up a short flight of steps, when a door opened before them. Carter instantly had his hand beneath his coat.

His fingers were just curling around Wilhelmina's butt, when he recognized Luís Braz's voice.

"Any trouble?"

"None," Leonora replied.

"Good. Let yourself be seen a little in the study window. I'll take him up the back stairs."

Carter heard the sharp click of her heels go down the hall as a door opened to his right. Pale blue light flooded the hallway where they stood, and Carter could see a series of tiny bedrooms on each side of the hall.

"Servants quarters," Braz explained. "Follow me up these stairs. We'll use Leonora's room. They're not so bothered by the shades being constantly drawn."

The room was massive, as Carter reckoned the whole house to be. A large brass bed, raised, dominated one entire wall. There was a sitting area along the opposite wall, in front of a fireplace.

Braz motioned Carter to a chair and took one opposite

him. A coffee table between them held a huge silver tray containing ice, bottles, and glasses.

"Whiskey . . . gin . . . brandy . . . wine?"

"A little whiskey would be fine," Carter replied.

"Ice?"

Carter smiled. Englishmen didn't dilute their whiskey with ice or water.

"Neat," he said. "President Tejada pays his cabinet members well."

Braz laughed with a guttural resonance. "Don't believe it. Tejada *is* the government. The government owns this house, and Leonora and I were assigned to live in it. Rent free, of course, but only because it is so much easier for his watchdogs to keep track of us here. As you have seen, there are only two entrances—front and rear—that they have to watch."

"And the servants' entrance?" Carter asked, accepting the proffered glass.

"That, as far as they know, only leads to the garden."

"Speaking of entrances . . . and exits . . ."

"Yes?"

"If that drainpipe won't hold me, I can't climb back up to that window. How do I get out of here?"

"We have that arranged. Cheers."

"Cheers."

A door opened at the far end of the room, and Leonora Braz entered.

She was even more beautiful in the light. She had shed the raincoat and now wore a sleeveless black dress that hugged every curve and hollow of her body.

Carter's eyes, over the rim of his glass, were impressed. She spotted it, and instead of averting her gaze, challenged him with her own eyes.

"Is something wrong, *senhor*?"

"Not a thing," Carter replied with a smile. "Do you always wear all black?"

"Yes, since the failure of the revolution," she replied.

"Leonora," Braz said, "will sit in on our little talk."

"Is that wise?" Carter countered.

"There are only four people in the world that I trust. My aide, Alex Dragos, a man named Miguel, another named Manuel, and my daughter. She knows all I know."

"Good enough," Carter said. "And I do know of Miguel Orantes and Manuel Ortez."

Braz grinned broadly. "Whoever you are, you have good intelligence and you have done your homework. As far as Tejada knows, Miguel and Manuel have been dead for two years."

Carter only smiled and pulled a thick folder of papers from his coat. But before he could speak, Leonora slid into the chair beside him and grasped his arm.

"We ran a check through British intelligence. They have never heard of Martin Harris-White."

"That is because he doesn't exist," Carter said icily. "Now, shall we get on with it?"

Luís Braz sighed and passed the last of the papers to his daughter for her perusal. Carter didn't speak as the older man removed his glasses and rubbed his eyes. Only when Leonora Braz finished reading did Carter lean forward and arrange the papers in separate piles on the coffee table.

"All very interesting and, I must admit, thorough," Braz said. "But a little farfetched and, I'm afraid, a bit of a maze to understand."

"It is all meant to be a maze, Senhor Braz, with no one except us knowing the way out."

Carter paused to let his words sink in, and then he

began, very slowly and very carefully, to explain.

"I gave this plan to General Fernandes in Paris. As you have read, it is a detailed outline of an almost foolproof way to topple Tejada. It is clever enough to work as long as Tejada doesn't know of its existence."

"But Tejada *does* know," Leonora said.

"Yes," Carter replied, placing his hand on the second stack of papers. "I explained this *counter*plan to Tejada in Miami."

"How?" Braz asked.

"In the guise of a Lieutenant Raul Moncada. The real Moncada is deceased."

Braz's eyebrows went up. "Then *you* were the reason Panama wanted me to trace all the Moncadas through our tax forms."

"Yes," Carter said. "Have you done it?"

"My aide, Dragos, has. There were four Rauls: two dead, a third about eighty, and the fourth a young boy of sixteen."

"We expected that. I want you to destroy the records on both the dead Moncadas. It will buy me the time I need. Now, shall I continue?"

"Please do," Braz said with a wave of his hand.

For the next hour, with a typed page in each of their hands for reference, Carter went over the details of the third—and master—plan for the overthrow of President Tejada's government and the elimination of Pablo Fernandes.

By the time he had finished, both of his listeners were leaning far forward toward him in their chairs, listening raptly.

"Dear God, it's the wildest scheme I have ever heard," Braz said at last, shaking his graying head from side to side. "Outrageous."

"Completely insane," Leonora Braz added, her eyes level with Carter's in a penetrating gaze. "But possible!"

"Very possible," Carter said. "And foolproof."

"That remains to be seen," the older man said and sighed. "Who will assassinate Tejada, and how?"

"I will do it myself, and that is the one part of the plan you don't need to know . . . either of you. The 'accident' will happen, I assure you, and it will be much better if neither of you knows the details."

They fired questions at him rapidly and in turn.

"How do we know we can trust you?"

"You don't."

"What do *you* have to gain out of all this?"

"Money."

"Who are your backers . . . your superiors?"

"I have none, and if I did, their identities would be kept secret."

And finally, after a last, long look at his daughter, Luís Braz again leaned forward in his chair and asked the question that Carter had been waiting to hear.

"And if we don't agree to this, what then? What will you do?"

Carter slipped Wilhelmina from her holster, jacked a load into the chamber, and set the Luger by his right hand on the coffee table.

"Then I will be forced to find another replacement for Tejada and go ahead with the plan anyway."

"But you could not do that without killing me and my daughter."

"No," Carter replied, lightly fingering the Luger, "I couldn't."

"You would do that? Kill us both?" Leonora cried, bolting to her feet.

Luís Braz didn't move from his chair. His eyes stayed

locked for a full minute on Carter's before he grasped Leonora's hand and pulled her back down to her seat.

"It doesn't matter, my dear, because we will go along with this plan."

"Then you agree?" Carter asked, relaxing.

"I do."

"To everything . . . including the money?"

"I do."

"Good. Here is a key. It belongs to a locker in the central train station. In the locker is a special radio and other equipment you will need when the time comes. There is also an envelope detailing every move I want you, Senhor Braz, and your people to make during the last twenty-four hours before the strike. Tell no one anything until that time."

"You think some of my people are disloyal?"

"I don't know, but I don't want to take any chances. Now, how can I contact Manuel Ortez?"

"You will have to go to him," Braz said, "in the mountains. He would be shot on sight in Rio."

"Then I will need a guide, one you can trust."

Again father and daughter exchanged quick glances.

"Leonora will take you. When?"

"A week from tonight." Carter turned to the woman. "Where is he?"

"In the jungle, inland from Bahia."

Carter nodded. "Can you trump up a good excuse to go to Bahia?"

"I can make one for her," Braz said. "Official business as my secretary."

"Perfect," Carter replied. "I will meet you one week from tonight. Shall we say ten o'clock?"

"Fine," Leonora said. "On the outskirts of the black section of Rio is an old cathedral, Our Lady of Divine

Grace. Take the cable car. I'll meet you there."

"I'll find it." Carter turned back to Braz. "Now, did you have Lapita del Preda watched, as I asked?"

"Yes, and you were right. She is having a clandestine affair with the CIA man, Brandon Hall. He visits her three nights a week in her Leme apartment."

"How does he do that with Tejada's men watching her?"

"That's just it. They don't watch her. Tejada doesn't think it would be proper. He rules all of Brazil with an iron hand. It would ruin his ego to think that his mistress was unfaithful to him."

"And Carlos Panama?"

"Who knows?" Braz shrugged. "But I doubt it. If Tejada found out that Panama was spying on his mistress behind his back, he might have Panama's head."

"Is Hall there now?"

"He was . . . Leonora?"

While she moved across the room to the phone, Carter tore all the papers from the coffee table into strips and fed them into the fire.

As he watched the flames turn the papers into ashes, he spoke again to Luís Braz.

"I've told you that in the weeks to come I will assume many faces."

"Yes."

"As Raul Moncada, I have access to Carlos Panama's intelligence network. He has made it possible for me, as Moncada, to travel unimpeded, and has given me methods of identifying myself to the authorities."

"And you need some way to establish your identity to my people?"

"Yes," Carter said, turning his gaze to the older man. "Something that will identify me immediately and insure that my every order and request will be carried out without question.''

There was only a moment's hesitation on Braz's part before he nodded and left the room. He returned quickly and handed Carter a solid gold medallion.

''There are only five of these in the world. They were pressed long ago, when all of us were much younger and still had faith.''

Carter looked directly into the other man's eyes ''I'm here to give you back that faith, Luís Braz. I'll guard the medallion well.''

He slipped the gold piece into his pocket as Leonora moved back to them.

''Here is her address. Hall is still there.''

Carter memorized the address and dropped the slip of paper into the fire. ''Call your man back and pull him off. I'll take it from here.''

''You're going there?'' Leonora exclaimed. ''You're going to expose yourself to her, Tejada's mistress?''

Carter smiled. ''If my guess is right, there is more than an affair going on between Lapita and Brandon Hall. I think we can use that.''

''How?'' Braz asked.

''Two ways,'' Carter replied. ''One, I think we can obtain—through Lapita del Preda—the records on Panama and Tejada's private, overseas financial empire. Those could be very valuable to you, Senhor Braz, once you are president. Would they not?''

''Of course,'' Braz said and nodded. ''And the second reason?''

''It is more difficult to get close to Carlos Panama than it is to the president. When the time comes, it will be Panama who could possibly ruin our plan . . .''

''And when that time comes?'' Braz asked.

"I want to get close to him myself," Carter replied.

He did not have to elaborate. All three of them knew why he wanted to get close to Carlos Panama.

"Now, how do I get out of here?"

"We will leave for a late meal. All you have to do is wait until the two in front follow us. They always do. It will be simple for you to slip out."

At the door, Leonora lingered behind her father. "Martin Harris-White, or whatever your name is . . ."

"Yes?"

"My father trusts you. He is usually a good judge of people, so I will trust you as well. But if anything should happen to him, I and the others would kill you. I guarantee it."

"My dear lady, I also guarantee you that, if anything happens to your father, there will be no need to seek revenge. It will probably happen to all of us as well."

Lapita del Preda disengaged her naked body from Brandon Hall and gave his chest a gentle shove.

"You must go, darling, and I must bathe."

"Because you're dining with him?"

His voice and his face were like stone, and it wracked her insides when she was forced to nod. "Yes. It is as it must be."

"It doesn't have to be, Lapita," Hall growled. "I have connections everywhere in the world. I can—"

"Hide me? No, he would find me and would bring me back . . . or worse."

"Lapita . . ."

"Shhh, darling. Go now and dress. Please, Brandon."

"Very well."

He moved through the door, and she ran water for a

bath. When the tub was filled, she scented it and stepped in.

She had long, tapering legs, thighs only a little fleshy, and her stomach was still flat between her jutting hip-bones. Her body, at thirty-five, was as lithe and sensual as it had been at twenty-five, when Carlos Panama had first seduced her and then passed her on to his then general, Frederico Tejada.

The years did not show on the outside . . . only inside, on her nerves and brain. It had been almost ten years of hell.

And then Brandon Hall had come along.

It was different with him and had been from the very first. It had started out as only a dalliance, a change from an old man to a much more virile and vibrant younger one.

But then, imperceptibly, it had grown into much, much more.

And now it had gone too far.

"Do you love him? . . . Tejada, I mean," Hall had asked.

"I am his mistress, his whore," Lapita had replied. "Love has nothing to do with it."

"But you're a woman. You need more."

She had laughed mirthlessly. "The only 'more' I would ever get if I left him, darling, would be prison."

Lapita soaped her body until her arms and breasts were covered with lather, and she sighed deeply.

Even luxuriating in the bath paid for by Frederico Tejada, Lapita knew things would never be the same.

Soon she would have to tell Hall, for his own safety as well as hers, that they must stop their affair.

But it would be hard.

She knew that some inner core of her soul, some tiny

part of her being that was woman, had been touched at last by a man. Brandon Hall had kindled a flame in her body, and she wondered if it could ever be extinguished.

She was just wrapping a towel around her when the bell rang.

She glanced at the clock. Frederico's driver was not due for another two hours.

Brandon, she thought, *has forgotten something*.

"Yes, who is it?"

"It's me, Brandon," came the muffled reply.

The lock had barely clicked, when the door was thrust open and kicked shut behind the tall intruder.

Lapita started to scream, only to have a powerful hand cover her mouth. The man's other arm lifted her effortlessly and carried her into the bedroom.

Unceremoniously, she was dumped onto the bed, still struggling and still with the hand choking off all her breath.

"Lapita del Preda, I am a friend."

Still she struggled.

"I can bind and gag you, but I would rather sit and have a normal conversation. If you agree, nod, and I will remove my hand. If you try to scream then, I will very probably knock you unconscious before I bind and gag you."

She nodded.

The first thing she did when the hand was removed was claw for the quilt to cover her nakedness.

"I assure you, I'm not here to rape you," the stranger growled.

"Then why are you here?" she hissed, her Latin temper now overcoming her fear.

"To find out more than I already know about you. What

would Tejada do if he found out you and Brandon Hall were having an affair?''

"Who are you?''

Carter smiled. "You didn't blink an eye, Lapita. Do you know what that tells me? It tells me that Tejada, and probably Carlos Panama, already know about you and Hall.''

She went limp under the quilt. The breath left her body in a great sigh.

"You are from Brandon's government, aren't you?'' she said weakly. "I knew you would find out sooner or later. But it is not his fault, believe me. And he has told me nothing that would do your government any harm, I assure you.''

"But you have told Hall a great deal about Tejada, haven't you.''

Now there was fear. Was this tall, seemingly laconic man, *not* from the U.S. government? Was he in the secret police of Carlos Panama? She knew the little ferret did employ a great many foreigners.

"I will say nothing.''

"Then let me guess.''

By the time he finished speaking, Lapita was sitting bolt upright in the bed. The quilt had slipped until most of one breast was exposed, but she paid little attention to modesty.

"You would do this for me? You would free me of Tejada?''

"If you will do what I ask of you . . . in precisely the manner I tell you. And Brandon Hall must know nothing of it, ever.''

"*Senhor*, I would do anything to be free . . . anything.''

ELEVEN

BRASÍLIA: NOW

Brandon Hall peered through the glasses and spat in disgust. Out of the mountains to the north, he could see columns of men and tanks converging on the two main arteries leading into Brasília.

They would be the lead units in Fernandes's assault group.

It wasn't a large force. But it would be large enough if they had surprise on their side. Moncada's information had been correct. They were moving exactly as the lieutenant had said they would and with approximately the same strength.

Tejada's forces, trained by Hall and the four other men in his team assigned to the president, waited in ambush on the outskirts of the city. They, combined with the air power from nearby Cuervica Airfield, should do a wipe-out job in less than an hour.

But something was wrong; something smelled. Years in Korea and then 'Nam had given Hall a supersensitive nose for smelling out bad operations.

121

And this one smelled.

He cursed President Tejada for giving so much decision-making power to a lieutenant. There were too many flaws. If the air power were late, or if there were a fourth column lurking somewhere undetected, the entire government force would be caught in the open with their butts hanging out.

Then Hall remembered the tongue-lashing he'd taken from Tejada when he had suggested an alternate plan. Terrorist guerrilla tactics were needed here, not open-field warfare.

Tejada had screamed. "You are an advisor! How dare you question the loyalty and ability of my men! Your own intelligence was rotten. One of my own trusted men discovered this coup. Were it not for Moncada, I could be dead! Where would you get your precious oil then?"

Where indeed?

Hall's intelligence was much better than he was at liberty to tell the president. For weeks the supposedly quiet rebels in the hills had been gearing up for what could be an all-out assault. But where? And, most important . . .

Why?

Luís Braz was now a highly respected member of Tejada's cabinet. True, Braz was as much a powerless figurehead as the other cabinet members, but he was serving the purpose Tejada had wanted. He was satisfying the rebels that they had a voice in the Tejada government.

So why now, when Fernandes was planning his coup, did a leaderless, supposedly weaponless band of disorganized rebels suddenly start organizing again?

Hall didn't know, and Tejada hadn't given him the chance to find out.

He again cursed the country he was in, the job he was

doing, and the conceited egos he was doing it for.

But he had made certain preparations.

He turned, swinging the glasses to the south and adjusting them until he found the two Land-Rovers. If anything did happen, he planned on getting his crew into the safety of the jungle, fast, and from there back to Rio.

And then there was another thing bothering Brandon Hall, perhaps even more than the coup attempt and miniwar he was about to observe.

It was the letter Lapita had given him twenty-four hours before, in Rio. Right now it was burning a hole in his pocket.

But he had promised.

"Do not read this, my darling, until you are back in Rio. Promise me!"

So he had.

Now he wished he hadn't.

The posh Leme residential district was nearly deserted. Carter expected that it would be. Practically everyone in Rio would be on the beach watching the festivities.

It was one-thirty when he got out of the cab and paid the driver.

"If you're back here in exactly one hour, you'll have an airport fare. All right?"

"Sim, senhor. Any fare is good today. One hour!"

Carter watched the cab round a corner and disappear down the hill toward the beach. If the driver did not come back, a cab would still be easy to get on the nearby Avenida Atlântica.

But it would be better if Lapita del Preda didn't have to walk that far carrying her bags.

That sort of thing in Rio draws attention.

The street on which Lapita's swanky apartment house

stood was nearly empty. There were five cars parked on her block, but there were no limousines, and Carter didn't spot Carlos Panama's personal car, a black Lincoln Continental.

He walked across the street and checked the windows of the buildings on the opposite side.

No snoopers.

But then he didn't think there would be.

No, this would be a very delicate situation for President Frederico Tejada. He would want it handled by someone he completely trusted to be both thorough and discreet. And Tejada trusted no one as he did the deadly Carlos Panama.

Carter could almost hear the conversation between Tejada and Panama when Lapita's note was delivered:

"So she has truly deceived me, Carlos. She has found herself a foreign lover and would fly away with him!"

"She knows a great deal, Your Excellency. Perhaps it would be better . . ."

"I agree, Carlos. Do it yourself, and make it look like an accident . . . rape, perhaps."

"I'll take care of it during the festivities this afternoon."

"Do you think it is Hall? Have we made a mistake using Lapita to keep track of our CIA man?"

"No, Your Excellency. It is an Englishman. We have been watching him at his hotel. He will be taken care of as well. You can count on it."

Carter was about to light a cigarette when a late-model black Lincoln turned a corner two blocks away and moved, almost soundlessly, down the street.

The car came to a halt across the street from Lapita's building, and Carlos Panama stepped out. He checked the street both ways, then walked purposefully toward the wide, distinctive glass doors.

The power of the secret police, Carter thought. There was no doorman on duty. He had most likely been told to take his lunch break in the basement at just that time.

The moment Carlos Panama disappeared inside the building, Carter moved back across the street and let his eyes float up to the fifth-floor windows.

He waited five minutes. Ten minutes.

He began to think Panama wouldn't give her time to drop the bait that her lover was picking her up.

Then the drapes closed, and, for the moment, Carter dropped the rolling, shambling gait of Salvatore Bellini. He practically sprinted the half block to the building and darted through the glass doors.

The lobby was empty.

Disregarding the elevator, Carter took the stairs three at a time. He paused for only a few seconds at the third-floor landing.

Nothing.

He climbed the last two flights at a slower pace, letting his heels resound on the marble as he moved.

At Lapita's door, he adjusted the chamois sheath beneath his right sleeve that held Hugo and then hung the arm at his side as if it were crippled or broken.

Lightly he rapped on the door with his left hand.

It was opened immediately by a white-faced Lapita del Preda. Carter stepped through the opening and embraced her with his left arm.

"Lapita, *carissima*, everything is ready. Let us go."

"Salvatore, I . . ."

"Step aside," came the raspy voice from the center of the room behind her. "And shut the door."

The woman stepped aside, pushing the door closed as she moved.

Carlos Panama stood in the center of the room, a silenced Walther in his hand, its deadly muzzle moving idly back and forth to cover both Lapita and Carter.

"You . . . raise your hands!"

Carter raised his left arm, high.

"Both of them!"

"I cannot, *senhor*. My right arm is crippled."

"Crippled?"

Suddenly Panama was laughing, long and loud.

"Dear God, you whore, you mean this is your lover? At least the Englishman had some class! Who are you?"

Panama was thoroughly off guard. The long silencer of the Walther dipped as he handled the gun carelessly.

"I am the man, *senhor*," Carter replied, "who has come to kill you."

"Kill me? You, like your whore, are insane!"

The Walther came up slowly. Much too slowly.

Carter tensed the muscle in his right forearm. The spring in the chamois sheath released, and a split second later the hilt of the deadly stiletto settled in his palm.

Carter's only movement was the whiplash of his right arm.

The aim was perfect, and deadly.

Hugo's blade embedded itself in Panama's throat with barely a sound.

The Walther fell to the floor, and reflexively Panama's hands shot to his throat. They never reached Hugo's hilt as he staggered backward and then fell.

Carlos Panama was dead before he hit the carpet.

Out of the corner of his eye, Carter saw the woman's face grow even more ashen. When her mouth opened to scream, he clamped his right hand over her lips and yanked her to him with his left.

"What the hell's the matter with you? I told you I was going to kill him."

"I know, but . . ." she mumbled.

"But nothing! He would have killed us both! Do you understand?"

She nodded. "It's just . . . the knife, I didn't know how . . ."

"The knife is a stiletto and it's very quiet. Are you all right?"

"Yes."

"Good. Now give it to me again."

Lapita del Preda reiterated what she had told him before in her bedroom. Tejada had once boasted drunkenly that the real key to his power, his wealth in all places, was his watch.

It had taken almost a half hour of questioning that night for Carter to get out of her what she didn't know she knew.

Carter removed Hugo from Panama's throat, cleaned the blade, and then yanked up the man's left sleeve.

"Do they match?"

"Yes," she said, nodding. "It is the exact duplicate of Frederico's. He never takes it off, even in the shower."

Carter smiled. That night, she had told him that Tejada had said, "We keep the same time, Carlos and I. Our watches are always synchronized to the computer."

Frederico Tejada liked to be mysteriously cute when he was drunk.

Carter slipped the watch from the dead man's wrist. It was an elaborate, Swiss-made job, with an extra large face and back.

He hoped he knew why it was so large.

With the tip of Hugo's blade, he very carefully pried away the rear plate. When it was in his palm, he flipped it over and brought it closer to his eyes.

"Well?" Lapita asked, hovering at his shoulder.

"I think so. Do you have a magnifying glass? . . . a strong one?"

"Yes."

She hurried into the bedroom and was back in seconds, thrusting the glass into his hand.

Holding his breath, Carter carefully scanned the inside of the faceplate. He wouldn't know until he made the phone call, but he was fairly sure the engravings he was looking at were computer codes.

"Where's the phone?"

Carter quickly dialed the number Luís Braz had given him. The phone was picked up on the first ring.

"Ministry . . . computer room."

"Alex Dragos?"

"*Sim.*"

"This is the Englishman. Are you alone?"

"*Sim*, except for my operator. Do you have them?"

"I hope so," Carter replied.

For the next twenty minutes, he reeled off the letters and numbers engraved on the faceplate.

"Is that all of them?" Dragos asked.

"Yes."

"Good, let me read them back."

"Do it slowly. They're tiny and hard to follow."

At last Dragos was finished reading them back. Carter gave him the number and instructed him to call the instant they had cracked the computer.

"*Sim, senhor.*"

Carter lifted the Lincoln's keys from Panama's body and then paced, smoking.

It was fifteen minutes before the phone rang.

"Yes?"

"We have them: every company name, every account number, every penny."

"Good. You know where to take the printout. I'll pick it up there. Don't let anyone else lay eyes on it!"

"I know, I've been told."

"*Adeus.*"

"Long live the revolution!"

Carter could have done without that. He recradled the phone and checked the window.

The taxi was there. Nothing like a long fare to the airport to a greedy cabby.

"He's there," he murmured to Lapita. "How many bags do you have?"

"Just the one." She motioned to a small carry-on sitting by the door.

"Good. Here's your ticket. It's through Miami to Paris." Carter paused and withdrew a thin envelope from his coat. "Here is the bearer bond I promised. Between that one hundred thousand, your jewels, and Hall's retirement, you can start a new life. *Adeus.*"

Lapita touched his shoulder at the door, turning him.

"It might not be enough to hide us from Tejada's hunters, but I thank you for what freedom I will have until they find me."

She leaned forward and lightly brushed her lips across his cheek.

Carter smiled and kissed her hand.

"Believe it, because you're hearing it from one who knows, Lapita, but Tejada will not come looking for you."

He watched her leave, leaning against the doorframe, then he sprinted down the stairs much faster than it appeared his bulk would allow.

There were a few pedestrians in the street now, but none even came close to being one of Panama's goons.

A short walk, again in the rolling gait of Salvatore Bellini, took him to the Lincoln. The big car started easily, and seconds later he was driving well past the speed limit down the Avenida Atlântica.

By the time he reached the center of the city, he had passed through two roadblocks that had been set up for the festivities. He hadn't even slowed up for either of them.

It might not have been Carlos Panama driving the Lincoln, but every police official and army officer in Rio knew the car.

Carter had been waved through both roadblocks with a salute and a smile.

At the main intersection of Rua Ouvidor and Rua Miguel Couto, he drove behind one of the stalls in the huge flower market.

A swarthy beggar in rags, with a long, black, drooping mustache, pushed away from a wall and approached the car.

"Miguel Orantes?"

"Perhaps," the beggar said, his hand hidden beneath his ragged jacket.

Carter flipped the medallion from his watch pocket and dangled it before the man's suddenly wide eyes.

"You are the Englishman?"

"Braz should have told you that I have many faces. Here are the keys. The car will allow you passage to the train station without question. Your men are ready?"

"*Sim*, all over the city."

"Good," Carter replied, already moving away. "Have a good war."

He walked three blocks toward the uncongested hill roads above the city and hailed a passing cab.

"Taxi, senhor?"

"Sim. I would like to go to the Sugar Loaf. The first station, please."

"Sim, senhor, but that is a long ride. *Muitos cruzeiros."*

Carter leaned forward and dropped "a lot of cruzeiros" on the front seat beside the driver.

"If you hurry, by the outer belt it's exactly nineteen minutes."

The driver smiled down at the bills, and the cab lurched from the curb.

"For you, *senhor,* seventeen minutes."

TWELVE

BAHIA: TWO WEEKS BEFORE

There is something very special about a cathedral, particularly at night. In the candlelight and the hushed silence broken only by the low monotone of mumbled prayers, one never felt alone.

Carter was no different.

Kneeling in a pew halfway between the altar and the entrance, he felt more than God's presence watching him.

Sure enough, to his left, partially hidden by a pillar, a man openly watched him.

He looked like a laborer or a peasant from the mountains in a rumpled pair of white canvas trousers and a dirty, once white shirt. A large stomach protruded from over his belt, and beneath a mop of stringy hair his face looked sallow and unhealthy.

Carter checked his watch. It was 10:45. He had been in the church nearly an hour, and no Leonora Braz.

He was about to rise and stretch his cramped legs, when footsteps echoed from beneath the old wooden arches near the marble altar. A priest, as ancient as one of the disciples, stepped from the darkness into a halo of candlelight. Slowly, his wise old eyes surveyed the few praying: two old women side by side in the front pew, a young girl near them, a man in his sixties mumbling the loudest, and Carter himself.

The old priest moved down the aisle, stopping at each person, blessing them with the sign of the cross and a mumbled prayer.

At last he was in front of Nick Carter.

"Bless you, my son," he said in a low, controlled voice surprisingly strong for a man of his age. "You are not of this village."

"No, Father," Carter replied, feeling the strength in the old man's eyes draw his concentration.

"I thought not. I would say that, perhaps, you are an Englishman."

Carter managed to stop the corners of his lips from curving into a smile.

"Yes, Father," he whispered, "I am an Englishman."

"You are far from your country, my son."

"It has become a very small world, Father."

"You are Catholic?"

"No, Father, I am not. But I would appreciate your blessing, for I have sinned."

As the priest moved his open hand through the sign of the cross in front of Carter's face, his body moved closer, obscuring Carter from the pudgy man in the side aisle.

At the same time, his left hand darted forward and pressed a folded piece of paper into Carter's hand.

"Go with God, my son."

"Thank you, Father."

When the priest stepped aside, shuffling toward the

altar, Carter peered again into the semidarkness of the side aisle.

The man who had been so diligently watching him was gone.

In the rear of the church he dropped coins into the box and lit a candle. When it was mounted, he checked quickly to see if another watcher had entered, then he unfolded the note.

> You are being watched. Leave by the south transept and follow that path down to the village. I will explain. L.

Carter set the note to the candle flame. When it was all charred ash except for a tiny bit between his thumb and forefinger, he dropped it and moved down the side aisle.

Outside, a brisk warm wind had come up. Above, the stars were bright in a clear sky, and even though there was no moon, Carter had little trouble locating the path.

As he moved he activated the spring in Hugo's sheath, sending the stiletto into his right hand. He kept the blade low to his side as his eyes darted back and forth in the night.

It was about four hundred yards to the village proper. Halfway there, the man who had watched him so intently from the church aisle stepped into his path.

"*Senhor* . . ."

"*Sim*, Carter said, tensing the muscles of his right arm for a throw if it should become necessary.

"You have papers, *senhor*?"

"I have many papers," Carter replied. "What business are they of yours?"

"Everything in this village is my business, *senhor*.

Foreigners rarely come out this far from Bahia. This is a poor section. What would you find interesting here, *senhor*?''

"That, *senhor*, is none of your concern.''

For all his fat, he was fast. A standard, long-barreled .38 seemed to just materialize in his hand.

"I am the authority in this village, *senhor*. I would like to know what a *turista* is doing so far from Bahia and the big hotels this time of night.''

Even in the dim light, the white of his knuckle on the trigger could be seen clearly.

Carter could have killed him, but there was no need.

There was a deep canal alongside the path. The man had only taken three steps when, from the darkness of its bank, Leonora Braz emerged. She moved like a gliding, silent cat until she was directly behind the man.

Calmly her hands came up, holding a silenced Beretta.

The little gun hissed twice, barely barking in her hand, and the pudgy one tumbled forward to land at Carter's feet.

It was as if she had been shooting on a range. Both slugs from the Beretta had caught him in the back of the neck.

"You can shoot,'' Carter said calmly.

"Since I was ten. I am a revolutionary, remember?''

"Was it necessary?''

"Yes. He spotted me in the village this afternoon. That would have mattered little, except when you arrived. He would eventually have put us together.''

"Who was he?''

"His name is unimportant. His job was to inform the security police in Bahia of anything he thought suspicious. There is one like him in every village.''

"What now?'' Carter asked, sliding Hugo back into the sheath on his forearm.

"We dispose of the body," she said, making the Beretta disappear into a shoulder holster under her jacket. "You carry the heavy half."

Oddly, Carter was not surprised at her calmness.

True, the Leonora Braz he was seeing now was a far cry from the chicly dressed woman he had first met in the Rio town house. But this other Leonora somehow fit with this particular time and place as well as she had the other.

They carried the body another forty yards down the path before she spoke.

"This way."

Carter hadn't even seen the break in the trees until they started moving into it.

"What's in here?"

"His grave," she replied. "I've already dug it."

I see, Carter thought, making a mental note to be very careful in handling Leonora Braz.

The road was asphalt and had not been repaired since it was first built. It was dotted with crumbling potholes the size of craters, and wide cracks through which every kind of weed and jungle vegetation grew without hindrance.

"Where does this road go?"

"Inland from Bahia," she replied, skillfully guiding the bumping jeep around a washed-out section of asphalt.

"I can see that. But where does it lead?"

"Nowhere," she said with a smile. "It was a pet project of Tejada's when he was in charge of public works. Money was allocated for a superhighway from Bahia to Brasília. This is it."

Carter nodded. "And what wasn't spent went into Tejada's Swiss accounts."

"Who knows?" she said and shrugged. "It sure didn't go into the road."

Suddenly they rounded a curve and came upon a group of shacks that seemed to have been huddled in the deep shadows of the trees and abruptly leaped out to the road and the jeep.

Oil lamps burned through tattered shades in the windows of a couple of them, and Carter momentarily saw faces staring out. The moment they saw the jeep, the faces disappeared and the lamps were extinguished.

"Won't one of Panama's men spot us here?"

"No. We're right on the edge of the mountains, in the foothills. This is rebel territory. Panama's men don't venture this far into the interior."

A hundred yards beyond the shacks, the road abruptly ended. There was no sign, no warning, just a log roadblock and jungle beyond.

They were barely out of the jeep when an old man and a boy appeared with a donkey cart. On the cart were twenty or more chicken cages.

"Help us load them!" Leonora said.

Carter did, knowing that when the time came she would fill him in on what the hell was going on.

Neither the old man nor the boy spoke a single word during the transfer of the cages. When it was finally accomplished, the old man climbed, still wordlessly, into the jeep, turned it around, and roared off.

"He will return the jeep to Bahia and sell his chickens in the market," she said. "We will go the rest of the distance by cart. As far as we can, that is. The rest of the way, we walk."

The boy appeared at her side.

"We go?"

"*Sim.*"

Carter followed her lead and crawled under a pile of straw and rags in the rear of the cart.

All around him was the pungent aroma of chicken droppings, and he suddenly realized that they were hiding.

"We're hiding."

"Yes," Leonora replied. "We have to pass through two more villages before we hit the high mountains."

"I thought you said Panama's informants didn't come this far inland."

"They don't."

"Then why . . . ?"

"You told my father that the CIA man, Brandon Hall, was not to know of your existence."

"That's right."

"Why should Tejada spend his money to bribe informers in the mountains when the CIA people will spend theirs?"

"Oh . . . I see . . ." Carter murmured, realization finally sinking in.

A slight smile curved Leonora's lips. "Now do you understand?"

"Completely," he replied as the cart lurched forward.

The first light of dawn was just breaking when at last the cart bumped to a final halt.

Groaning, Carter uncoiled his long legs from the bed of the cart and jumped to the ground.

They were halfway up the side of a densely forested mountain. A sliver of sun over its peak sent an eerie saffron glow through the trees and illuminated a narrow, rocky path.

"Now we walk?" he asked.

"We walk," Leonora answered and she turned to the boy who was wheeling the cart around. "*Obrigado*."

The boy didn't speak or smile as he climbed back into the seat of the cart. Just as he sat down, his thin coat parted and Carter saw the butt of a .45 automatic protruding from the waistband of his peasant trousers.

"Something wrong?" Leonora asked, seeing his concentration on the boy as the cart lumbered away.

"The forty-five," Carter replied. "Does he know how to use it?"

"Of course. He's a crack shot."

"How old is he?"

"Eight," she said, shouldering a pack and handing a second one to Carter.

Carter shook his head as he watched the cart disappear from sight, then he turned to Leonora. "Where do we walk?" he asked, shrugging the straps over his shoulders.

"Up there."

Carter looked up to the very peak of the mountain.

It looked to be about a hundred miles away.

It was a one-room shack with scant caulking in the cracked walls and a tin roof. There were two windows, but they had been boarded up years before.

"Who owns it?" Carter asked, sliding the pack from his back and rubbing the welts the straps had caused beneath his jacket and shirt.

"Government," Leonora replied with a smile. "Ironic, isn't it? They own the whole mountain and everything on it, and we're going to use it to meet Manuel Ortez."

There was a single cot with a thin blanket thrown across it, an old-fashioned chamber pot beneath it, and a stand with a huge, ancient Zenith radio. The only other furnishings were a few rickety chairs and a table.

From her pack, Leonora took two packages of dried beef, a loaf of bread, and a bottle of wine.

"Hungry?"

"I could eat the table," Carter said, pulling up two of the chairs.

She rummaged in a shelf on the wall and returned with two cracked cups. Carelessly, she tugged the tail of the plaid shirt she wore from her jeans and cleaned them. As she poured the wine, Carter broke the loaf of bread in half and split the dried beef.

Like a man, Leonora threw her leg over the back of the chair and sat down to tear ravenously into the food.

"You're used to this, aren't you," Carter said, doing justice to the food himself.

"What . . . living like an animal, you mean? Yes, it's part of the training."

"I'm surprised."

"Oh?"

"Your father was the intellectual, the political head of the revolution. He wasn't in the hills fighting."

"I was. I fell in love when I was fifteen. He was a revolutionary. My father wanted me to stay with him at the university in Rio, but when the fighting broke out he knew I wouldn't."

"So you went into the hills with your lover."

Leonora nodded slowly. "Eventually. We were married. He was captured three years ago, not far from here."

"And . . ."

"They executed him. Firing squad."

She said it as if she were giving Carter the latest weather forecast.

They fell silent, each with his own thoughts, as they chewed the dried beef and bread, and sipped the wine.

It was several moments before she spoke again.

"Manuel and the others will be here around midnight. In the meantime, we should rest. We will take two-hour watches."

Carter nodded his agreement. "All right. I'll take the first."

"You're sure?"

Carter smiled. "I've had my share of jungle fighting and survival. Believe me, I'm not tired."

"Very well."

She stood, stretched her tall, lean body, and crossed to the cot.

Without an ounce of modesty, false or otherwise, she shed her jacket and then stripped off her boots, shirt, and jeans.

"You can see every trail up the mountain from each of the windows," she said, paying no attention at all to Carter's staring eyes. "The boards are nailed loosely. Wake me if anyone comes before your two hours are up."

"I will," he replied, unable to remove his eyes from the wealth of her breasts as they spilled from the cups of her bra.

The panties slid over her hips and off her long legs as quickly and easily as everything else. Then, nude, she faced him.

"If you want coffee, there is some in my pack."

"Thank you."

"Is anything wrong?"

"Not a thing. You have a beautiful body."

"Thank you."

She slid onto the cot and carelessly tugged the blanket over her. As she turned to the wall, Carter lit a cigarette and rose to pull his chair toward one of the windows.

"Englishman?"

"Yes?"

"You're not English, are you."

"No."

"Then why are you doing this?"

"I told you," Carter replied, his eye rolling over the swell of her hip under the blanket. "Money."

"I don't believe that any more than my father does."

"Then let's just say I have a love of danger, and I like adventure with rebels and beautiful women."

"That may be possible," she replied, her face still to the wall. "But hardly reason enough."

Carter dropped the butt to the floor and crossed to the cot. He reached down, found her chin with his fingers, and rolled her around to face him.

Slowly he leaned down and grazed her lips with his before releasing her and resuming his full height.

"If you have to have a reason, Leonora, then think on this one: you have a cause, I have a job."

"And what is your job?"

"Killing people."

Carter wasn't surprised when her full, sensuous lips curved into a smile.

"That," she said, "I can understand."

They were seated around the table: Carter, Leonora Braz, Manuel Ortez, and a hulking giant that Ortez had introduced only as Joaquim.

Candlelight flickered off their stern but rapt features and only partially illuminated the open map beneath their eyes.

"*Senhor*," Ortez said, his lips barely moving, "what you are asking is not impossible, but it is very suicidal."

Carter smiled through the haze of cigar and cigarette smoke that hovered above the table.

Ortez was tall, taller and leaner than Carter himself. He had a long, sardonic face, and his thick black hair was starting to recede in time with the flecks of gray that had begun to sprout along the temples.

Carter guessed he was only about thirty, but years of jungle fighting and mountain living had etched their way into his face and left their scars on his black eyes.

All in all, Carter liked him.

"It can be done, Manuel," Carter said. "The big question is, do you have enough pilots left from the old days to fly the planes after it is done?"

Ortez leaned back in his chair, expelled a thick cloud of cigar smoke, and shrugged.

"I have them. They are rusty, but I think they can carry out the plan you propose." Here he paused and smiled. "After all, they were trained by the best in the world . . . the United States Air Force."

"Then I see no problem."

"The communications at Cuervica Airfield are excellent. At the first sign of trouble, they can call reinforcements that would shatter my men in less than an hour's time."

"Then we knock out the communications first."

"And the guard detachment there is one of the most highly trained Tejada has."

"I've told you how that is to be accomplished," Carter replied.

"That is what bothers me. This Lieutenant Moncada has the names of officers at Cuervica loyal to Fernandes . . . right?"

"Right."

"These officers, at the right times, will capture Tejada's Marines in their own barracks . . . right?"

"Right. Then your men will, in turn, take over the Fernandes men and control the base. With any luck, not even a shot will be fired."

"Sounds plausible," Ortez said, shrugging again. "But if we are to meet you in Cuervica to supervise the planting of the explosives, *and* Moncada to rendezvous with Fernandes's man, where is this Lieutenant Moncada?''

Carter stood and moved to his pack. He extracted a uniform tunic, a shirt, and a pair of trousers. The tunic had the insignia of an army lieutenant.

Carter returned to the table. He laid the clothing across the map, and then withdrew two documents and placed them on top of the uniform.

"I am Raul Moncada."

Ortez didn't bat an eye, but he did exchange a quizzical glance with Leonora Braz, who only shrugged.

He scanned the documents, then looked up at Carter with a frown.

"These are very powerful documents."

"They are," Carter agreed with a smile. "Officers of any rank, loyal to either Tejada or Fernandes, will follow the orders of the man who holds them . . . no matter if he is only a lieutenant."

"One is signed by Fernandes and one by Tejada. You mean—"

"Moncada," Carter replied, "works both sides of the fence."

Suddenly Ortez laughed, a raw, harsh laugh that came from deep in his gut.

"You are a very special man, Harris-White . . . or whatever your name is."

"Does that mean you agree?" Carter asked.

"Why not?" Ortez replied, pushing his chair from the table and rising. "We have nothing to lose."

"And a country to gain," Carter said, lifting the uniform and documents from the map. "The timer and charges you will need are in my pack. I'll leave them with you."

"And the frequencies?"

"Here." Carter passed a piece of paper to the other man. "When I arrive at Cuervica for my inspection tour, I will make sure that these four areas are completely clear during the noontime hour."

"It will be risky in the daylight . . ."

"Nothing is not risky in a revolution, Manuel," Carter said "You of all people should know that."

"*Touché*. I and my people will be there."

"Good. One week from tomorrow. I'll be coming in by helicopter from Rio. Watch for it. The moment I land at Cuervica, have your people in place. Agreed?"

"Agreed. Joaquim."

The hulk grunted, stood, and moved to his leader's shoulder. Ortez held out his hand. Carter took it, and both men smiled.

Then Ortez turned to Leonora.

"You go back to Bahia tomorrow afternoon?" She nodded. "Good. Both of you can sleep well tonight. I will leave two of my men on the path at the bottom of the mountain."

"*Obrigado*."

Carter had already folded the map. He passed it to Ortez, then rescued the oilskin-wrapped packages and a black plastic box from his pack. These he gave to Joaquim.

"Plastique?" the big man asked, cradling the packages like a brood of infants in his massive arms.

"*Sim*," Carter said, "but very special plastique . . . very concentrated. The detonators are already set to the frequency on the send unit."

"One week from tomorrow," Ortez growled, and both men moved to the door.

The hulk passed through, but Ortez paused and turned.

"Leonora . . . ?"

"*Sim?*"

"One moment?"

She nodded and followed him from the shack.

Carter lit a cigarette and refolded his pack after putting Moncada's uniform back inside it.

By the time he had finished, Leonora had reentered the room.

"Hungry?"

"No," Carter said.

"Then we should sleep. It will be a long hike again tomorrow."

Carter nodded and extinguished all but one of the candles as she began unfolding a bedroll from her pack.

"You can take the cot."

"No, thanks," he replied. "I'll use a bedroll, too. If I'm going to be able to sleep all night, I'll do it much better on the floor."

"Suit yourself."

He spread out his own bedroll and managed to keep his eyes averted as Leonora went through the same undressing ritual he had already witnessed once before.

By the time he looked her way again, her clothes were piled neatly on the floor and she had slipped into the bedroll.

Carter undressed himself, extinguished the candle, and, clad only in his underwear, lay down.

"Leonora?"

"*Sim?*"

"What did Ortez tell you . . . outside?"

There was a full minute of silence before she replied in an even, calm voice.

"He said that if anything, even the slightest thing went wrong at Cuervica, he was giving Joaquim instructions to blow your head off."

Lying on top of his bedroll, Carter smiled.

More silence.

This time a full five minutes passed before she spoke again.

"Doesn't that bother you, Englishman?"

"Not in the least."

"Why not?"

"Because nothing will go wrong."

She rolled around to face him, raising herself on one elbow. A thin shaft of moonlight from a crack in a window passed over part of her face and one exposed breast.

"But if something does?"

"Then I will be gone, not there for Ortez or Joaquim to kill."

"And them . . . Ortez, Joaquim, the others . . . ?"

Carter shrugged in the darkness.

"They will have to die, and we will have to change the plan."

"Englishman, you are a cold son of a bitch."

"I know."

A smile of pure warmth caressed Leonora's full lips. "And that is why I like you. Only someone like you could make this work."

"Thank you."

Another pause, then, "Do you still think I am beautiful, Englishman?"

"Yes."

"Is it true what they say?"

"What is that?"

"That all the English are cold lovers?"

"I wouldn't know," Carter replied. "And, besides,

I've already told you I'm not English. Remember?''

"Would you like to make love to me?"

"No."

One eyebrow shot up and the smile faded from her lips. In the darkness, the grin on Carter's face widened.

Slowly he reached his hand out and let his fingers trail along the full side of one breast.

"But," he growled, "I would like to have sex with you."

Each could feel and sense it in the other. Both had meant it to be lust, pure sex.

Where it changed, where in the course of coming together it had become something more, Carter couldn't remember.

From her breast he ran his fingers up to curl in the thick silk of her hair. At the same time, her hands deftly tugged at his shorts until they were gone.

Then a tremor ran through his body as her hand returned to the inside of his thigh.

"You are a beautiful animal," she whispered. "I have admired your body."

Her fingers felt like five tongues of flame as they moved upward, branding the skin of his thigh. At last they closed around their objective, bringing a startled gasp of pain and pleasure to Carter's lips.

He reached for her hungrily.

"No . . . wait . . . slowly," she whispered. "It will be so much better. We have the night. Let us use it."

Thoughts of the long trek down the side of the mountain the next day faded as her grip tightened and her fingers began to piston over him.

Instinctively, he began to move his hips, matching the rhythm of her strokes.

Then, suddenly, her touch was gone. His eyes flew open, searching in the beams of moonlight sifting through the boarded-up windows.

She stood above him, her full lips red and wet, her back arched to thrust her full, naked breasts to the light.

She was the most beautiful, lascivious thing he had ever seen.

"Well?"

"If you mean, am I ready? . . . yes," he replied. "Is there much doubt of it?"

Her eyes danced to his crotch. They seemed to smolder as they devoured his nakedness. And then she reached with one foot and tugged her bedroll until it met his.

"Good," she breathed. "Now make me ready."

She seemed to float, even glide, rather than fall onto the floor beside him.

He kissed her, his teeth catching at her lower lip. Gently but firmly he sucked her lips, then her tongue, into his heated mouth, her breath hot against his face as guttural moans rolled from her throat.

At the same time, his hand found the gentle roll of her belly. Her thighs parted and her own hand guided his to the moist tangle of her pubic hair.

As he broke the kiss, she squirmed herself over his fingers and guided one of her breasts to his mouth.

"Yes, yes," she moaned, "like that, just like that . . . feels so good!"

Half crazed now, Carter started to roll on top of her. He was halted by her hands on his chest, pushing him back.

"No . . . let me."

She swung one leg across his body and straddled him.

Suddenly Carter chuckled.

"What is it?"

"I was just wondering what your father would say."

"He would say nothing, Englishman," Leonora sighed. "He knows I am my mother's daughter."

She positioned her buttocks on his thighs. With deft, heated fingers she found him and raised herself.

Then, with a groan of ecstasy, she lowered herself slowly until she was impaled to the root of his desire.

They began to move, separately at first, and then as one.

The tempo increased, and then increased again.

Somewhere, far off, Carter heard her shriek her fulfillment. Her body arched and tensed over him.

When it relaxed, he carefully turned her over until he was above her, sliding smoothly like a machine between her damp thighs.

Twice more she shrieked, and then Carter himself exploded.

Gently he dropped his matted chest to her breasts and then rolled to her side. Leonora came with him, planting gentle, biting kisses on his forehead and eyes.

"Beautiful," he sighed, "very beautiful."

"Sleep, Englishman, sleep. I will wake you just before dawn."

"Before dawn?"

"Yes. That is the best time to make love."

THIRTEEN

RIO: NOW

Carter left a very happy cabdriver at the base of the first station. He slipped into the crowd easily and waited in line for a cable car ticket.

Behind him, Sugar Loaf rose majestically against the sky. Beneath him, Rio, Copacabana Beach, and Guanabara Bay lay like a shimmering jewel.

"One."

"*Sim*," a bored attendant replied, shoving the notes into a drawer carelessly and pushing a ticket toward Carter through a hole in the wire cage.

He moved with a knot of people into one of the cable cars, and positioned himself in a far corner as the door was slammed and the car started its steep ascent.

A few people got off at the intervening stations.

Carter rode all the way to the top.

Most of the remaining people moved on up the mountain toward the restaurants and recreation areas.

Carter found the path he had already checked out and moved down it toward the more dangerous—and thus less traveled—area on the bay side.

Eluding the tiny knots of people watching the festivities down in the bay, he finally found himself alone.

But even then he didn't stop. He moved farther among the rocks until he could not be seen at all from above.

At last he found the solitary spot beneath a rocky overhang that he had pinpointed days before. By skidding and sliding on his well-padded butt, he managed to submerge himself even further into the rocks and brush until he was completely hidden from any random eye.

From where he sat he had a clear view of the presidential car pulling into the Ilha das Cobras and the massive form of the tanker inching its way toward the center of the bay.

Off came the jacket and the pants. From the sheath on his right forearm came the stiletto with its razor-sharp six-inch blade and narrow handle. He squeezed the handle, and the hilt, curved and padded to fit his fist for close-in fighting, snapped out and locked in place.

One slice of the blade ripped the spare-tire padding in the trousers. Another opened the padded back and shoulders of the jacket.

He removed a small radio send-receive unit, no bigger than a hardcover book, and a miniature HF-DF scoop. Two rods driven into the earth held the scoop as he attached a battery and watched it slowly start to rotate. He switched the radio unit on and rolled the knob to "receive."

A barely audible beep came from the tiny speaker and then died away as the scoop moved away from the bay.

Carter took some bearings. The wind was light, and it originated from the southeast. That was good. He was prepared for it, and the unit on the yacht was operating perfectly. He made some adjustments on the scoop until the beep from the speaker became a steady, pulsating hum.

Satisfied, he pulled cold cream, tissues, makeup, false sideburns with a gray tint, mustache, and a tiny contact lens box from the coat.

With the aid of a pocket mirror he worked quickly and deftly to change Bellini into a dapper English gentleman with a pencil-thin mustache, only slightly but maturely gray. The dark, brooding eyes now flashed gray.

The hum was constant now, much stronger than necessary. Carter reached over and flipped the knob to "send," and again settled back to enjoy the splendor of the peaceful view of Rio from Sugar Loaf Mountain.

There was only an hour to go.

Luís Braz alighted from the car and moved quickly around to the other side where a uniformed officer was standing at rigid attention.

A huge roar went up from the assembled masses as the president emerged. Tejada stood to his full short height, planted a wide, plastic smile on his face, and waved to them.

Here and there Braz could easily spot the men Panama had planted in the crowd to lead the cheering.

The yacht, the *Lapita*, bobbed against rubber tires at the end of the pier to Braz's right.

He smiled. It was ironic that Lapita del Preda's name was still on it. Tejada would dearly have loved to rename his new toy before today's celebration, but there had not been time.

The roar of a plane came to Braz's ear above the cheering of the crowd.

His eyes lifted, and there, slanting into the blue-domed
sky above the bay, was a Boeing 747.

Braz almost chuckled.

It was the Miami flight.

Idly, he wondered if Lapita del Preda was looking down
through one of the plane's windows at her strutting, bemedaled former lover.

What a shock she would have when she landed in
Miami and found out the true events of this day, and
realized what part she had played in them.

"Luís . . . ?"

"Sim, meu Presidente."

"Where is Carlos? I don't see him. He was to meet us
here at the pier."

"I don't know, *meu Presidente.*"

"Well, damnit, find out!"

Luís Braz dove back into the car, fingering a small
piece of paper from his pocket. Using the limousine's
direct phone line, he dialed the number on the paper.

A voice answered on the first ring.

"Sim?"

"Dragos?"

"Sim."

"Luís." His eyes rolled up to look through the limo's
windshield. He couldn't see the phone booth on the corner
four blocks away, but he knew Dragos was there.

"Is it done?"

"Sim," Dragos replied. "We are in charge of all security on the beach and the pier. Nothing can go wrong
now."

"And the car . . . Panama's Lincoln?"

"We have it, Luís," the voice replied gleefully.
"There is no roadblock we can't go through in Rio!"

"Good. Five minutes."

"*Sim, meu Presidente,*" Dragos replied.

"Not yet, Alex," Luís Braz replied with a smile. "Not yet . . . but soon."

He reset the receiver on the cradle in the console and slid back out of the car.

"*Meu Presidente . . .*"

"*Sim*, Luís?"

"Carlos has been detained at the train station . . . a security matter."

"Damn. Well, we cannot wait!"

"No, Your Excellency. Your speech."

"*Obrigado*," Tejada said, taking the rolled sheets from Braz and turning toward the pier. "We go aboard!"

Tejada marched away, his uniformed entourage falling in step behind him.

Luís Braz fell into the end of the line. When they were nearly to the pier, Braz sidestepped toward the crowd. At the last second, he ducked under the restraining ropes and began elbowing his way through the mass of humanity.

It took him nearly three minutes to reach the Avenida Atlântica, so he had to break into a run when he reached the open area.

"Easy, easy," Braz whispered to himself as he trotted toward the train station. "Don't overdo it now. Don't have a heart attack when you have . . ."

He rolled his wrist upward until he could see the face of his watch.

". . . when you only have fifty minutes to go."

Clutching the briefcase in her hand, Leonora Braz slid from the seat of the tiny Fiat and made her way across the street.

Above her loomed the tiered concrete walls of Maracana Stadium. To her right, as she reached the curb, was a tiny café.

She entered and ordered a glass of wine. When it came, she sipped it, laying the briefcase on the table and crossing her arms over it.

How ironic, she thought. In a few minutes a revolution would be taking place all around her and, through it all, she would be sipping a glass of wine.

But she didn't feel left out.

Inside the briefcase beneath her arms was the future of her country.

She felt odd about passing it over to the Englishman when he arrived, but those were her father's orders.

Her eyes dropped to the briefcase. Suddenly they misted and an odd choke slipped into her throat.

The Englishman . . . who wasn't an Englishman.

She remembered the night on the mountain.

Like two animals they had attacked one another, again and again demanding—and receiving—pure physical pleasure, ultimate release, until at last they had fallen, exhausted, to each other's side.

Then they had slept.

Just before the blue of the moonlight had started to fade and be replaced by the first fingers of orange dawn, she had awakened him.

Gently, ever so gently, he had taken her in his arms.

It was then they had made love.

In the new light she had looked up into his eyes and seen the difference. Gone was the crisp, hard coldness. They had softened. Now they looked at her as a man should look at a woman.

And she had returned that look, with her eyes and with her body.

Leonora Braz had had many men, but none had fulfilled her so much as that man had that morning.

And no man had ever looked at her that way.

She ran her hand over the briefcase and wondered if she would ever see that look in another man's eyes.

Her father's instructions from the night before drifted into her thoughts.

"There has been a change of plan, Leonora. Dragos will meet me at the pier. I don't trust anyone, not even Alex, to deliver the briefcase to the Englishman."

"But I thought Dragos would deliver the briefcase himself to Brasília."

"No. Without the briefcase, the Englishman might decide to forego his final payment and find his own way out of the country."

"But with the briefcase, he will meet the helicopter . . . and you."

"Yes. He must go to Brasília, Leonora. He must."

It was then she knew what they planned on doing.

Her eyes became even wetter.

But her spine straightened.

They had made love and it would be hard for her to forget it.

But forget it she would.

She was a revolutionary, and the cause of her country came first.

"Senhorita . . ."

"Sim?" Leonora replied, rolling her wide eyes up to the waiter's jovial face.

"More wine?"

"Yes . . . yes, bring me a bottle of the best."

"Ah, a celebration, yes?"

"Sim," she said. "It is a day for celebrating."

FOURTEEN

CUERVICA AIRFIELD: THE LAST WEEK

"Lieutenant Moncada?"

"*Sim*, Colonel."

Carter stepped from the helicopter runner and surveyed the man before him through very dark glasses.

Colonel Octavio Ramos was about forty-five years old with brush-cut blue-black hair under his garrison cap. He had the sincerest black eyes Carter had ever seen, coupled with heavy-jowled features that made him look downright noble.

Another Tejada or Fernandes, Carter thought, *waiting in the wings*.

Carter saluted and handed over the prized letter of introduction from President Tejada.

"Highly irregular, but under the circumstances that Secretary Panama has acquainted me with, I can certainly see the point. Lieutenant, my base is at your disposal."

"Thank you, Colonel."

"May I present my air commander, Major Lopes."

Carter saluted. "Major."

The two men exchanged knowing glances as they shook hands. There was puzzlement in the major's eyes, but Carter would do away with that later.

Major Lopes had long wanted Colonel Ramos's rank and job. By being loyal to General José Fernandes, he was sure he would soon get it.

The puzzlement was that Major Lopes had expected a blond-haired man with a scar, a man named Lindeman.

"It is near noon, Colonel," Carter said. "I would like to brief all the men in your main mess hall."

"All?"

"Yes, Colonel . . . even your sentries."

In the nearby jungle, Manuel Ortez rubbed his hands in glee.

How the Englishman had done it, he didn't know. But that was unimportant.

He had.

The entire base, away from the mess hall, was deserted.

Through his field glasses Ortez could see his men slithering on their bellies from place to place, planting the charges.

Slowly he reached down and patted the black plastic box at his side.

The tower would go first, then the communications shed. Next the armory would blow, so that if they did put up a fight, they wouldn't have its tall, thick concrete walls to fall behind and make a stand.

Lastly, the narrow pass that led off the plateau would cave in, blocking the one road in and out.

Even if something went wrong and somehow word got out, there would be no armed reinforcements coming up that road.

"Good God," Ortez whispered, patting the black box again, "what a blow it will be!"

It was dusk.

Carter had stood in front of the full complement of the air base—132 officers and men—and explained the coup in detail.

All were amazed.

He had finally managed to assure them that there was nothing to worry about, that the president knew of the coup and that all precautions had been taken.

Their main job was to have the full complement of Sabres ready to take off at a moment's notice should they be needed.

Colonel Ramos had been convinced.

Now it was Carter's job to convince Major Lopes that everything he had said was bullshit.

But what he was about to tell *him* was gospel truth.

They entered the tiny but well-appointed hut, and Lopes gestured him to a chair.

"Drink?"

"Beer," Carter said. "After such a long-winded speech my throat is dry."

The major opened an apartment-sized refrigerator and withdrew two bottles. After opening them, he passed one to Carter, eyeing him guardedly.

"I must say, Lieutenant Moncada, you were very eloquent."

Carter met his gaze. "And, for the most part, truthful."

"Oh? . . . And what wasn't the truth?"

Carter passed the official document across to the major and added a second piece of paper, a personal letter from General Pablo Fernandes.

Lopes read it, reread it, and looked up with a smile.

"The planes will be ready, Lieutenant, on this date. But you can tell the general that they will never leave the ground."

"Good," Carter replied, leaning forward. "How many men can you trust?"

"All the pilots, of course. And almost all of the ground crews."

"Can you arm the ground crews the night before, and just before dawn have them take the Marine barracks?"

Lopes nodded enthusiastically. "Child's play. Over half of them will be sleeping. I can arrange for free beer the night before in the enlisted men's mess. That should guarantee it."

"Good," Carter said, rising and extending his hand. "If all goes well, Major, our futures are insured."

"Give my best to the general," Lopes murmured.

"I will. Your very best."

Carter had been sweating. Convincing both sides that he was on both sides had been a very tricky proposition.

It still might not work at the last minute.

But by the last minute, it would be too late.

The engine of the copter was warmed and the rotor was already starting to turn as he settled into the rear bucket seat and snapped the belt over his lap.

At five hundred feet, the big machine heeled over and headed south-by-southeast.

Carter held his breath . . . waiting.

And then he saw it, about a mile north of the base, deep in the jungle.

A powerful flash came on three times, paused, and then came on three more times.

The signal was repeated, but Carter was no longer straining his eyes to see it.

It was done.

The charges were laid.

Tejada's men would think it was civil war.

Major Lopes and his Fernandes contingent would never know what hit them.

And Ortez would fly.

FIFTEEN

RIO: NOW—THE COUP

Nick Carter took one last, long pull on the cigarette and let the smoke ooze lazily from his distended nostrils.

Finally he crushed the fiery tip against a rock by his foot and then shredded the butt.

The tobacco was dribbling from his hand in the light wind, when his attention was captured by the explosion of distant cheering in the bay.

Its source was the throats of three hundred seamen lining the deck of the monstrous supertanker. In seconds the cheering was augmented by the brassy strains of a military band.

Under his breath, Carter hummed a little tune. It meant nothing, but it kept his fingers away from the firing box.

The behemoth ship had settled near the center of the bay now, its engines idling, holding it steady to await the boarding of its owner.

A boarding, Carter mused with a smile, that would never happen.

His gaze moved landward, toward Copacabana Beach

and the nearby piers. From Carter's vantage point, the big yacht moving into the bay from the line of piers was no more than a gleaming white ant.

He moved the set of high-powered binoculars to his eyes, adjusted them, and smiled even more broadly.

Even from such a distance, the glasses easily picked up the glint of the sun reflecting on the gold-visored hat and the chest of gleaming medals.

Even in the mass of gilt-laden uniforms, he would be the one with the most gilt and the most medals.

President Frederico Tejada stood proudly with his officer corps on the yacht's flying bridge, awaiting his moment of glory.

The fingers of Carter's free hand played idly over the two buttons on the book-sized console.

It was all happening just as he had guessed. The yacht's skipper was keeping a slow, steady pace of about five knots.

Tejada would go to any lengths, Carter thought, to achieve the dramatic for those watching along the shore.

When a third of the distance to the tanker had been reached, Carter dropped the field glasses to his chest.

From his coat pocket he extracted a pair of earplugs and dark sunglasses. These in place, he again checked the beams, going and coming, on the tiny scope.

From the remnants of Bellini's clothing, he took two rocket skids and one of the the two rockets. He anchored the skids into the ground and then set the rocket in them, adjusting the clamps so it would blast off without interference.

With a turn of a switch on the rocket, the batteries became activated. Then it was only a matter of adjusting the frequency between the rocket detonator, the bomb on the yacht, and the firing console.

Satisfied, he moved his finger to the left side of the console and gently depressed the black button.

The hum from the speaker became a whine. The detonator was activated.

There was only the red button left.

Manuel Ortez stood on the concrete apron in front of Cuervica Airfield's hangars and stared in awe.

It had all happened so quickly and easily that Ortez felt as though he should pinch himself to make sure that the moment was real.

To his right, standing carelessly and cockily hipshot, were the eleven fighter pilots under his command.

Directly in front of him squatted the twelve castoff American Sabre jets that made up the inland command of President Tejada's Air Force.

All twelve of the jets were armed, fueled, and ready to roll.

And to his left was the real center of his awe. Standing in a clustered circle and guarded by a motley, ragtag group of barely clothed, heavily bearded rebels, were the forty Marines who had been the guardians of Cuervica Airfield. Another group of dazed Marines and enlisted men were penned up in the barracks, also under rebel guard.

Behind Ortez, tied together with one length of rope and looking foolish standing with downcast eyes in only their underwear, were the twelve pilots who normally flew the Sabres for the president.

Somewhere at the far end of the compound, a burial detail was taking care of the six men killed during the brief attack.

Among them were Major Lopes and Colonel Ramos.

Just as they had been told, the operation had taken less than twenty minutes. If the rest of the operation went according to the Englishman's plan, twelve years of struggle, defeat, and living like moles in the mountains and jungle would soon be over.

Ortez turned to his men.

"Ready?"

The affirmative replies resounded in his ears.

"All right. May God smile on our cause and help us, after all these years, to remember how to fly these damned things!"

President Frederico Tejada felt his chest swell and his legs quiver as the yacht drew closer and closer to the giant tanker. Even his mouth went a little dry when he thought of the millions of barrels of oil resting in the supertanker's huge holds.

Oil?

No. Pure gold.

And all his.

Four more years of power, and he, Tejada, would be one of the richest men in the world.

His whole body quivered when his eyes fell on the gaily colored bunting of the speaker's platform aboard the tanker. It was high above the main deck on the superstructure and seemed to beckon him. The entire superstructure had been draped in his honor.

And then another quiver—this one having nothing to do with muscles or nerves—flowed up his spine.

President Frederico Tejada had not survived all these years without instincts. And suddenly, at that very moment, his instincts were speaking to him, warning him.

But of what?

He looked around the bridge, and the faces he saw stared back at him. They were smiling faces. And why shouldn't they be?

All the men on the bridge were his coconspirators in his grand plan to rape their country. They, as well as Tejada himself, would profit greatly in the four years to come.

And then his ears were filled again with the loud cheering of the men on the tanker's decks. It was quickly followed by a chant from the multitudes lining the beach.

"Tejada! . . . Tejada! . . . Tejada!"

He scoffed at his own fears.

He moved to the front of the bridge and unfolded the pages that held the speech he would soon deliver on the tanker. It was the speech that would tell his people and one third of the world about the new era he was about to create in Latin America.

The sheets were blank.

His forehead furrowed into a scowl, and he swiveled his head in search of Luís Braz. The fool.

What was Braz trying to do?—Embarrass him? He would have the bastard's butt for this. Braz had given him the wrong papers!

Where was he?

And then Tejada felt frightened again. He was sure that Luís Braz had been right behind him when he and the rest of his entourage had boarded the yacht.

"*Meu Presidente*," an aide asked, "is something wrong?"

"Wrong . . . ?"

"You are pale, Your Excellency, and your hands are shaking."

Tejada was about to answer, when the deck beneath his feet began to rumble. The vibrations started at his heels and moved clear up through his spine. They were followed by a low rumble somewhere in the bowels of the yacht.

Tejada's mind whirled.

My God, he thought, *we've run aground! But how in hell can we run aground in the middle of the bay?*

Braz.

Luis Braz, that son of a bitch!

The rumbling sound grew, and the whole ship shook. Suddenly there was pandemonium on the deck in front of him. Tejada turned his anger toward the captain.

But before he could utter one word, he felt his body being lifted as if by some giant hand. He was flying and just above him, more than six feet from his body, was a human leg.

Then he realized it was his own leg.

President Frederico Tejada realized nothing else, not even his own death.

Carter kept his finger on the red button. He knew it was no longer necessary, but he somehow felt better, more a part of it, touching the reason for it.

His eyes behind the glasses were sad, but his powerful will and determination kept his mind a blank.

He watched the guts of the yacht, almost directly under the bridge, erupt hundreds of feet into the air. He could also see the antlike bodies fly apart, but, out of necessity, he saw them as only one body: Frederico Tejada.

The blast shattered windows over a mile away and filled the air with a rolling rumble that would dwarf the thunder of the rainy season. More, smaller blasts followed as each succeeding fuel tank in the yacht exploded.

It was only a matter of time, a very short time.

As the two halves of the sleek white pleasure craft slipped into the waters of the bay, Carter became a blur of motion.

From the padding that had made Bellini's girth, he withdrew the second rocket. This one was shorter and fatter than the first. Its center, from the cone back to just short of the firing and fueling mechanism, was hollow.

Quickly he mounted the rocket on the skids and slanted it toward the chaos still taking place in the bay.

All of the equipment he had thus far used went into the center of the rocket pack. Once that opening was closed and secured, he locked the whole into place.

On the back of the pack was a flat plate with several spring clips. Carter inserted the console into the clips and made it fast. The scoop and tripod were attached to half of a double row of clips along the top of the pack. Quickly he removed the earplugs and dark glasses. They found their way into Bellini's clothing, and the whole bundle was attached to the remaining row of clips.

He set the timer for three minutes and scrambled up the rocks to the top. He moved down the path sideways, pointing and gesturing in the direction of the bay, much the same as the awed people he deftly passed among.

To random questions, at him or anyone in general, he gave random answers, always in perfect Brazilian Portuguese.

Later, if anyone remembered the rocket blasting off, no one would remember a foreigner among them on the mountain.

Finally free of the crowd, Carter moved quickly down the path toward the cable car. Most of the people trying to get down were families.

He had already reckoned for this.

It would be a chance in a million that anyone would be stopped and questioned. But if any one person was, it would be a solo man.

Carter took no chances, not even one in a million.

He let two cars leave, then he spotted a woman with three small children and a picnic basket. She was frightened, the children were frightened, and she didn't have enough arms.

Again he spoke in perfect Portuguese.

"Por favor, senhora. Let me help."

He scooped two of the children into his arms and quickly deposited them in the cable car.

"Obrigado, muito obrigado!" the grateful woman said.

Next came the third child, and then he helped the woman aboard. In seconds they were moving down the mountain, the woman mopping her brow, one child crying against her voluminous breasts, Carter idly bouncing her other two offspring on his knees.

He turned back in time to see the rocket pack streak off toward the sea. It wouldn't be identified among the debris from the yacht. It was important that nothing be found on Sugar Loaf or anywhere else in Rio other than the Swede's suitcase.

"A dreadful day, *senhor,*" the woman declared. "Dreadful."

Carter nodded. "Indeed, terrible," he agreed. "But be glad the sun still shines on us."

On nearby Corcovado's 2,330-foot peak stands the world-famous statue of Christ the Redeemer. The statue is to Rio what the Eiffel Tower is to Paris.

On this day it was the perfect observation post for Luís Braz.

Through a pair of high-powered glasses, he watched the yacht explode, break into two pieces, and begin to sink into the sea.

His eyes glazed. He had not been told how it would happen, only when.

"In the bay," he had been told. "Just climb to the

statue, take the glasses, and watch the bay. Believe me, Luís Braz, it will happen.''

And it had.

"Jesus," he whispered. "The bastard Englishman—if he is indeed an Englishman—has done it!''

He scrambled from the statue's tall base and ran to where Dragos waited.

"Is it done?"

"It is done," Braz replied. "Signal Fernandes's forces to attack.''

Alex Dragos made the sign of the cross and switched on the power of the portable transmitter the Englishman had given them.

The two men looked solemnly at each other, almost as if they could hear the radio beam as it flew inland to Brasília and General Pablo Fernandes.

"May God forgive us," Dragos whispered.

"God?" Braz replied. "No, Alex, let Him forgive *them*. They will need His forgiveness more than we.''

Brandon Hall felt bile rise in his gut. He swallowed several times to keep from vomiting. No one, Lieutenant Moncada in particular, had mentioned the two Russian-made attack helicopters. They were slicing the Tejada lines to pieces.

And beyond the scope of the helicopters, Fernandes's and Tejada's ground troops were cutting each other to ribbons.

"What do you think, Hall?"

"I think it's a lost cause. Where the hell is the damn Air Force?"

"Can't reach 'em. Control at Cuervica doesn't answer.''

"Bastards," Hall hissed.

"What do we do?"

"What the hell else can we do?" Hall replied. "Let's get the hell out of here. You know as well as I do, it's no fun getting caught on the losing side!"

"Jesus, Brandon, I don't think we have to worry about that. From the looks of it, there ain't gonna be a winner . . . just losers."

Hall had to smile.

Tejada and Fernandes beating the hell out of each other.

It couldn't happen to a better pair of bastards.

General Fernandes watched the two assault helicopters pounding rockets and machine-gun fire into Tejada's troops along the northern commercial sector. The troops that he could see and a few splinter groups along the foothills were the only remnants of Tejada's commandos.

The Swede was right.

How he had done it, Fernandes neither knew nor cared, but the Sabre jets had never shown up.

It had been a slaughter.

Along with hidden tanks on the ground, Fernandes had brought in his surprise weapons: the helicopters.

Three sweeps in a direct attack with machine-gun fire from the copters, and the line was broken. Following that, Tejada's commandos had lost almost all of their heavy equipment with the first wave of rocket fire.

Tanks and heavy mortar fire from his infantry had further decimated the enemy's numbers.

Now ground troops were cleaning up.

The radio crackled.

"For you, *meu Presidente*," the pilot said, smiling as he pulled off the earphones and handed them over.

Fernandes tried to keep his hands steady as he adjusted

the phones over his ears. It was equally as hard to ignore the surge of joy in his gut brought on by the man's words.

"General . . . ?" came the faint voice through the static.

"*Sim*."

"It is done. Tejada is no more . . ."

Fernandes pulled the earphones from his head. The man was still talking, but the general had heard all he needed to hear.

"Take it down," he said. "On the roof of the Palácio. It is over."

Had General Fernandes listened to the rest of the man's excited speech from the Rio end, he would have learned that heavily armed rebel troops were pouring into the city.

Every word that Fernandes hadn't heard, Manuel Ortez *had* heard, sitting on the runway of Cuervica Airfield, with the powerful tremors of the Sabre gently rocking his body.

He smiled and shook his head. It was happening. It was really happening.

He switched channels and depressed the microphone button at his throat.

"Leader to Group, Leader to Group . . . in fours . . . let's go!"

General Fernandes's helicopter touched down on the roof of the presidential residence, the Palácio da Alvorada, just as the two Russian aircraft settled onto the green lawns of the esplanade below.

His elation knew no bounds as he unbuckled himself from the seat and made his way to the door of the copter.

Tejada was no more. He, Fernandes, would soon be the sole leader of the party and his country.

But he would give the old president his due.

A statue, perhaps.

Yes, that was the least he could do. When the time came, he would give them the proper show.

But at that moment, he must capture the reins of government, must inform the people that he was now their president.

They would grow to love him . . . someday. And those that refused would die. It was the generals and the Army first—get them to support his claim—then the people.

Just as Fernandes stepped from the door of the copter, he thought of returning to the radio with one question: Had Luís Braz been on the ship with Tejada?

But the Russian, Zeimov, was tugging at his elbow. "I must get to a radio . . . my superiors . . ."

"Yes, yes," Fernandes hissed and turned to an aide. "Take him below . . . to the radio room."

Then Fernandes moved across the roof to survey his city, his thick gut sucked in as far as it would go, his chest swollen with pride.

The tall, dapper man with the pencil-thin mustache and graying sideburns helped the children from the cable car and accompanied them to the street.

After many thank-yous and a farewell, he walked away from the woman and her children with long, purposeful strides.

It was relatively calm in the area where he walked. Most of the chaos and fighting was near the plaza, the bay front, and around the two train stations.

He would be going nowhere near that area.

Three blocks of walking took Carter to the parking lot

used by customers of the various small businesses around Sugar Loaf and the cable cars leading up the mountain.

It was three-quarters full of cars, bicycles, and Vespas.

He walked down the line, examining each of the small motorbikes with a careful eye. At last he chose one and knelt to pull and twist at the wiring.

Two minutes later he was riding the highway toward Maracana Stadium.

He looked like an English gentleman on his way to work, who had opted to ride his Vespa that day and leave his Jaguar in the garage.

Brandon Hall instructed his driver to pull into a service area fifty miles from Brasília on the highway to Rio. The other Land-Rover swerved in and parked behind them.

"We'll wait it out here and head on into Rio tomorrow. Whatever this damned war is about, it looks to me like it's gonna be a short one."

"Great. What if the Russians have invaded?"

Hall smiled and moved away from his men, tugging Lapita's letter from his pocket. "Then we'll just have to wait until we're repatriated, won't we?"

Carefully, he broke the seal on the letter's envelope and unfolded it.

My dearest Brandon,

Don't ask me how it has happened, because I cannot tell you. I hardly know myself. It just has. Darling, I am free. We both are. By the time you read this, I will be on my way to Miami, and from there to Paris. You always said that one day you would take me to Paris, that we would walk the Seine like young lovers and make love in the most elaborate suite the Ritz has

to offer. I'll be in that suite, my love, waiting for you. Hurry to me.
All my love,
Lapita

He had barely finished the last line before he was sprinting back to the Land-Rover.

"Mount up, we're moving on!"

"To Rio?"

"You damn betcha!" Hall cried.

"But there's liable to be a war there, too, man."

"I don't give a shit. I've got a report to file and a plane to catch. Move your asses!"

Fernandes stood on the roof of the Palácio da Alvorada and stared out across his city, his capital, his Brasília.

It had never looked more beautiful.

He was glad that the pompous, boorish Russian was below, out of the way. He had brushed his aides aside as well.

This was a moment he wanted to savor alone.

He could not control himself. A peasant yell erupted from his chest, and he pounded the stone balustrade with his fists in glee. He moved his eyes along the rows of buildings as though he had never seen them before.

The architecture astounded him. Why? Beause Brasília was a city of the future.

He would make it *his* future.

Were he a religious man, Pablo Fernandes would have fallen to his knees and prayed.

So intent was he on his revelations that he hardly heard the roar from the mountains to his right. Somewhere on the periphery of his consciousness, the sound built, came closer and closer. . . .

His dreamlike state was quickly shattered by stark reality when the two Russian helicopters disintegrated on the esplanade below.

Just as quickly, he saw the rebel troops streaming from the jungle.

Not his own troops, nor those of Tejada's . . . but rebels.

Luís Braz's ragtag mountain army.

And then the roaring above him lifted his red-rimmed eyes.

The sky was filled with the sound of jet engines as he looked up. They were in groups of four.

One set strafed his troops while another backed them up. And still a third set started a wide arc that would zero their rocket launchers in on the roof of the Palácio . . . the roof where he stood.

The Swede had lied, or he had fouled up.

Damn the Swede!

Around him was chaos as his officers and men tried to get the helicopter started in time. But Fernandes was an old soldier.

He knew there wasn't time.

The screaming engines of the jets filled the air.

And then the Sabres were in place, starting their dives.

Fernandes's eyes rolled toward the heavens to see a second, then a third sun in the sky.

They were bright, burning, and trailing vapor. And they were stationary. They were hurtling directly at the spot where he stood.

General Pablo Fernandes never knew the truth.

In the second before the roof exploded and his body was incinerated, he still thought that, somehow—even in death—it was Tejada who had defeated him.

Even as the grounds of the Palácio itself swarmed with the rebel troops of Luís Braz.

Carter abandoned the Vespa in a parking lot and walked the last few blocks to the stadium.

He was just short of the entrance when he saw her.

She was sitting in a café, calmly sipping a glass of wine, her arms crossed over a briefcase. There was a half-full bottle of the red liquid at her elbow.

He was about to ignore her and move on, when she openly motioned him to join her.

Both the street and the café were empty.

He didn't like it, but he moved in under the awning.

"So we meet again after all." Her voice was slightly slurred and there was an odd, vacant expression in her eyes.

"It would seem so. Has the copter landed?"

She nodded. "About fifteen minutes ago. I heard it."

"Then I had best . . ."

She dropped some notes on the table, grabbed the handle of the briefcase, and fell into step beside him.

"I'll tag along."

"To Brasília?"

"What if I said yes, to Brasília . . . and even beyond that?"

"I would say, go back to your bottle of wine."

"I thought you would."

There was an odd catch in her voice that almost made him turn his head. But at the last second he checked the impulse.

They turned into the main entrance of Maracana Stadium and moved through the huge, vaulted arches. In the near darkness of the tunnel, Leonora clutched his sleeve and brought him up short.

"Look at me, Englishman."

Slowly, Carter turned to face her, lowering his right arm and barely tensing his muscles. From long practice, he could feel the spring in Hugo's chamois sheath tighten just short of the point of release.

"This morning you said good-bye to a fat little Italian man named Bellini. You should have left it at that."

"I couldn't," she replied, taking one of his hands and closing it around the handle of the briefcase.

"The computer printouts?"

She nodded. "My father wants you to take them to Brasília."

"Why?" he asked, his eyes slowly darting to and fro in the darkness of the tunnel.

She shrugged. "Orders. That's all he told me."

"You're sure?"

Her eyes lowered, averting his. "He said they would be safer with you in the copter."

Carter relaxed. He smiled and used the index finger of his free hand to lift her face back up to his.

It was in her eyes. He could read it like he could read the lines in his own palm.

But he said nothing.

Instead, he leaned forward and pressed his lips hard to hers. The kiss was brief. When he heard a tiny sound in her throat and felt her body move toward his, he lifted his lips and stepped back.

"Good-bye, Leonora Braz . . ."

"Then, you're going . . . to Brasília?"

"Yes," he replied, glad that it was too dark for her to see the knowledge in his eyes. "I'm going to Brasília, Leonora. And don't worry, I'll be going beyond."

He left her there, standing in the darkness, and moved on through the tunnel.

Above clicking heels, he worked his way through the concrete structure of the largest football stadium in the world. In moments the heels became silent as he stepped out onto the grassy field.

In the center of the field was the helicopter, its rotors gently turning in the sun. He approached the machine slowly, not wishing to alarm the rebel officer or the soldier beside him.

They were both armed, the soldier with a stubby M-16 pointed directly at Carter's chest.

"You are here for a good reason, *senhor*?" the officer asked.

"I have business in Brasília. I believe you are running a special taxi service." His words were clipped and elegant, precise in his English enunciation.

"Perhaps you are correct, *senhor*," replied the officer, lowering the .45 in his hand. "I was told you would have a certain object for identification."

Carter nodded and tugged Luís Braz's medallion from his pocket.

Idly, he swung it before the officer's eyes as he moved toward the open door of the helicopter.

Bijorn Lindeman couldn't believe this was happening to him.

The tall, blond Swede wanted to blame Bellini. Surely the fat little Italian had betrayed him, informed on him to these men who identified themselves as agents of the new government under Pablo Fernandes.

But within minutes, the tables were turned.

His captors were themselves arrested by members of the rebel army. And the rebel officer—Miguel, he called himself—was declaring Bijorn Lindeman a political prisoner.

But he wasn't a political *anything*.

He was a smuggler.

But should he tell them that? Which was worse . . . the truth, or a lie he couldn't invent?

Bijorn's small mind couldn't comprehend such swiftly changing events.

"But I am innocent!" he cried. "Innocent!"

"Innocent of what . . ." Miguel Orantes glanced down at the passport in his hand. ". . . Bijorn Lindeman? I haven't accused you of anything yet."

"I am . . . I am innocent of anything." Even to Lindeman's dense mind his words sounded hollow.

Orantes sneered in response.

He dug his hands into the briefcase and threw the contents onto the floor. With deft fingers, he peeled away the covering inside the top. Bundles of currency tumbled out.

"How does an innocent, jobless merchant seaman come by so much money, Bijorn Lindeman?"

"Diamonds. I sold some diamonds."

Orantes flipped the case until it rested, bottom side up, on the table. A knife from his belt slashed at the leather until the bottom compartment gaped open.

"And what are these?" Orantes asked, holding a tiny tape recorder in one hand and a black, book-sized box with a red and black button on its face in the other.

Orantes smiled. "I think, Bijorn Lindeman, that you are indeed a political prisoner, and the charge against you will be sabotage."

"No, *no!*" the Swede cried through quivering lips, sweat running from his face. "It's Bellini! He's short and fat and—"

"Take him away."

The sight of the yacht exploding in the bay swam before

Lindeman's eyes. The thought of being charged with the assassination of a president wrenched at his guts.

This was too big for him to handle. Smuggling, petty theft, even the murder of another small-time criminal . . . prison for those charges didn't frighten him.

But sabotage and political assassination? The only sentence would be death.

With a scream of rage and fear, Lindeman broke free of the hands holding his arms. His feet propelled him headlong across the station toward the trackside doors. He would lose himself among the cars and eventually in the chaos of the crowded city.

His fleeing body was framed in the sunlight streaming through the open doors when Miguel Orantes's pistol cracked behind him.

Years of close fighting in the jungles had made Orantes an expert marksman. The bullet entered the skull at its exact juncture to the spine.

Bijorn Lindeman was dead before he hit the ground.

Luís Braz got out slowly from the command car and made his way across the tarmac toward the waiting presidential jet.

His step was plodding, and his red eyes were blurred with fatigue.

But he was happy.

In one day he had accomplished what he had been struggling to achieve for twelve years. Twelve bloody years of fighting and political intrigue.

Luís Braz was president of Brazil

The radio communiqués from Brasília had given him a detailed description of Fernandes's death, and the ultimate disruption and capitulation of his forces.

As the Englishman had foretold, the "divide, conquer, and destroy" theory had succeeded.

"*Meu Presidente*," said Miguel Orantes at his side.

"Luís, Miguel . . . it's still Luís. You and I were in the jungle too long together for it to be anything else."

Miguel nodded and his face broke into a knowing smile. "You'll need these."

"Yes."

Luís Braz took the tape recorder and send-receive unit from his friend's hand, and stored them in the briefcase he carried. The case also contained the Seal of State, one million American dollars, and a pictureless, nameless passport.

He had barely fastened the belt across his lap when the jet started to roll.

Minutes later, they were at twenty thousand feet, heading straight inland over the jungles that had spawned a rebellion and, for so long, hidden the man who now flew above them.

The first jolt of the wheels on the runway brought Luís Braz awake. Quickly, he went to work shifting the money and the passport into a second briefcase. The task was completed by the time the plane rocked to a halt.

He carried a briefcase in each hand as he deplaned and walked the few steps to a waiting field car.

"Palácio da Alvorada," he said. "Home of the president."

The driver grunted and the car sped away. Two motorcycles and another car preceded them, while an armored weapons carrier bristling with machine guns brought up their rear.

Luís Braz smiled, almost sadly.

It was the way of the world. Such preparations and precautions were necessary. How futile it would all be if he were assassinated before he could even take the oath of office.

He forced himself to ignore the chaos around him as they entered the city just as he had ignored his conscience when the Englishman had come to him with the plan to make him president.

It was a daring, almost impossible scheme, and many lives would be lost. But the man had given him, Luís Braz, the choice: a despot for a despot, or the elimination of them both and his ascendancy.

And the scheme had worked.

The caravan rolled to a halt before the ruins of the Palácio.

Braz's mind was already seething with plans. He would have to rebuild his government, solidify his political base, soothe the angered opposition he would encounter, and renegotiate the oil contracts that Tejada had given away for personal profit.

But one more meeting had to be concluded first.

Braz stepped from the car even before it had come to a complete halt. A smiling Manuel Ortez, still in his flight suit with his helmet under one arm, awaited him.

"Welcome to Brasília, *meu Presidente*."

"Well done, Manuel," Braz said, "well done."

The two men embraced and then stood staring into the depths of each other's eyes.

"It has been a long time coming, Luís."

"Let us hope not too long, my friend."

The sound of a helicopter reached their ears.

"That will be him," Braz said, leading the way toward the front lawn of the building.

They had just stepped around the corner when the

chopper settled onto the grass. The rotors continued to spin slowly as the door opened and the tall man in the Savile Row-tailored suit jumped lithely to the ground.

The man strolled toward them with a brisk, confident step. The thin mustache on his upper lip followed the slight smile. The gray, penetrating eyes that Luís Braz remembered so well were now obscured by dark glasses.

"President Braz, you have my congratulations."

The new president eyed him, trying to see beyond the cold reserve he saw in the face. "I hope congratulations are in order."

The man shrugged. "It is your country now. You have the tape and the detonator?"

"Yes. The Swede is dead," Braz replied.

"Good. Transition will be smooth. My conversation . . . as the Swede . . . with Fernandes will prove that the general assassinated Tejada. You will be a good leader, Luís Braz."

Braz chuckled. "And if I am not? You'll come back . . . and I'll be next."

There was no reaction, not even the twitch of Carter's mustache to reveal that he had heard Braz's words.

Braz handed one of the two briefcases to a guard and, retaining the second one, moved toward the helicopter. Ortez and two of his bodyguards fell in behind him.

Braz waved them away.

"*Meu Presidente . . .*"

Another wave of Braz's hand and the man fell silent.

The two of them fell into step as they moved toward the copter.

"You have Panama's papers?" Braz asked.

"Yes." Carter lifted the briefcase he held and pushed it into Braz's free hand. "I assume you were the one who gave her the orders to give it to me."

"I was," Luís Braz replied, straining to see behind the heavily tinted lenses.

He couldn't. And it worried him.

Somehow, the Englishman knows.

Dear God, Braz thought, *does he know* everything?

"With those," the taller man said, "a great deal of Brazil's money can be returned to the people."

Braz nodded. "Let us hope I don't ever have to use the knowledge in these papers to keep my office. The people would never trust another politician."

They walked a few more steps in silence before Braz spoke again.

"Who are you?"

"You know my name."

"I know *a* name . . . Harris-White. It is false. Who are you really? And who do you represent? Surely—"

"Does it matter, Luís Braz?"

"I have a right to know. You have given me a country . . ."

Suddenly the dark glasses were off, and Luís Braz was staring into the coldest pair of eyes he had ever seen.

"I've given you nothing, Luís Braz, but an opportunity. Use it well!"

Braz nodded.

He stopped, and Carter stopped with him. After a few seconds of deep concentration, Braz spoke again.

"I don't like you or your methods, but I can't help but admire you."

He handed over the briefcase he had been holding originally.

In turn, Carter pressed the medallion into Braz's hand.

"I have no more use for this."

Carter turned and walked the remaining distance to the chopper. The pilot stood in the door waiting for him.

There was a sudden tug at Braz's elbow. It was Ortez.

"Should I give the signal?"

"What?" Braz said, staring at the tall figure jumping from the ground into the open bay.

"The signal. Should I give the signal to have him killed? It is all arranged with the pilot, as you suggested."

There is no truth and honesty in the world of power, Braz thought. *Men who rise far above their fellow men to lead must protect themselves.*

This man, whoever he was, had almost single-handedly overthrown a powerful government.

If he had done it once, he could do it again.

"Yes," Braz sighed. "Kill him!"

Manuel turned and raised his arm.

The pilot's hand, holding an automatic, came up from the side of his leg.

But before he could fire, cloth and a burst of flame and smoke flew from the pocket of the Savile Row suit.

The pilot fell to the floor of the copter with a scream of agony. The gun fell from his hand as he clutched his shoulder and writhed.

Almost gently, he was pushed through the door to sprawl on the ground.

"I didn't kill him, Luís Braz. But always remember that I could have."

As the door closed, Braz saw the tall man's hand lift in a salute.

In seconds, he was at the controls and the chopper was lifting into the air. It whirled once in a complete circle, then headed west.

Braz watched it until it became a dot on the horizon and then disappeared.

"*Meu Presidente,*" Ortez said, gently touching Luís Braz's arm.

"*Sim*."

"I could radio the airfield. One of the Sabres could catch him in minutes before he gets out of our airspace."

"No," Braz replied, shaking his head. "What would be the use? That one is a man who expects death. I can sense it. Let him find it in his own way, and in his own time."

The new president turned on his heel and walked toward the bombed Palácio.

What happened to the rest of the world, he thought, and the part this stranger had in causing it, was of little concern to him, Luís Braz.

He now had his own country to run.

DON'T MISS THE NEXT NEW
NICK CARTER SPY THRILLER

DEATH HAND PLAY

Carter turned away from the stairs and followed the corridor to the front, where he stopped again to listen in the shadows at the foot of the main staircase.

A grandfather clock chimed the half hour in the living room to the right.

The study, where he had seen Rojas hand over the money to the other two men, was to the left. Entry was through a set of double doors with wide brass hinges, long door handles, and a very large, ornately tooled lock.

It took Carter under a half a minute to spring the two-hundred-year-old lock with his stiletto, and he pushed open the doors, stepped into the study, and silently closed and relocked them.

There was little or no light in the study. Carter took out his penlight, aimed it in the general direction of the desk, and flashed it on.

He got the brief impression of a large man, seated behind the desk. His arm was coming up, when Carter's penlight went out. Carter rolled left, diving for the floor.

The characteristically soft plop of a silenced weapon sounded twice, once to the right where Carter had been and the second just inches away from Carter's right leg as he rolled once again, then lay perfectly still.

Carter slipped his stiletto out of his sleeve, then held his breath as a rustle of fabric came from behind the desk. A floorboard creaked, then was still.

For what seemed like a very long time, Carter remained lying where he was, not moving a muscle. The other man was doing the same. He was a professional. In the brief moment Carter had seen the man's face, he had recognized him as one of the two Rojas had handed the money to: short cropped hair, weather-beaten complexion, the look of a hard man. And now this.

It would not be long before the dawn came, and then this game of hide and seek in the darkness would be over for both of them. It would become increasingly difficult for Carter to get out of the house, and return to his car without being detected.

The entire operation could go down the tubes at this point, if Rojas knew for a fact that Carter was something other than he presented himself to be. If someone saw him leaving this place, and could identify him, Rojas would bolt.

Which meant one thing. The man across the desk was going to have to die. And within the next minute or so.

Carter turned his head toward the door, cupped his mouth with his free hand, and coughed once. In the darkness even a pro would be fooled by the direction of the sound.

The gunman fired two shots toward the door, the muzzle flash just barely visible through the silencer barrel.

Carter rose to his knees and threw the stiletto in that direction. The gunman grunted, then fired two more shots in Carter's direction, but Carter had swung farther left, and he ducked below the level of the desk.

Again the study was absolutely silent.

Carter had hit the man with the razor-sharp blade. He knew that for a fact. But it could have been a superficial wound, perhaps in the man's arm, or a leg.

He reached carefully inside his tuxedo for his Luger, and his pocket for the silencer. He was screwing the silencer on the end of the barrel when something hit the desk. He nearly jumped out of his skin.

—From DEATH HAND PLAY
A New Nick Carter Spy Thriller
From Charter in September 1984

☐ 71539-7	**RETREAT FOR DEATH**	$2.50
☐ 77413-X	**SOLAR MENACE**	$2.50
☐ 79073-9	**THE STRONTIUM CODE**	$2.50
☐ 79077-1	**THE SUICIDE SEAT**	$2.25
☐ 81025-X	**TIME CLOCK OF DEATH**	$1.75
☐ 82407-2	**TRIPLE CROSS**	$1.95
☐ 82726-8	**TURKISH BLOODBATH**	$2.25
☐ 87192-5	**WAR FROM THE CLOUDS**	$2.25
☐ 01276-0	**THE ALGARVE AFFAIR**	$2.50
☐ 09157-1	**CARIBBEAN COUP**	$2.50
☐ 63424-9	**OPERATION SHARKBITE**	$2.50
☐ 14220-6	**DEATH ISLAND**	$2.50
☐ 95935-0	**ZERO-HOUR STRIKE FORCE**	$2.50

Prices may be slightly higher in Canada.

Available at your local bookstore or return this form to:

CHARTER BOOKS
Book Mailing Service
P.O. Box 690, Rockville Centre, NY 11571

Please send me the titles checked above. I enclose _____ Include 75¢ for postage and handling if one book is ordered; 25¢ per book for two or more not to exceed $1.75. California, Illinois, New York and Tennessee residents please add sales tax.

NAME_____

ADDRESS_____

CITY_____STATE/ZIP_____

(allow six weeks for delivery.)   A8

☐ 14217-6	**THE DEATH DEALER**	$2.50
☐ 14220-6	**DEATH ISLAND**	$2.50
☐ 29782-X	**THE GOLDEN BULL**	$2.25
☐ 47183-8	**THE LAST SUMARAI**	$2.50
☐ 57502-1	**NIGHT OF THE WARHEADS**	$2.50
☐ 58866-2	**NORWEGIAN TYPHOON**	$2.50
☐ 65176-3	**THE PARISIAN AFFAIR**	$2.50
☐ 71133-2	**THE REDOLMO AFFAIR**	$1.95
☐ 71228-2	**THE REICH FOUR**	$1.95
☐ 95305-0	**THE YUKON TARGET**	$2.50
☐ 13918-3	**DAY OF THE MAHDI**	$2.50

Prices may be slightly higher in Canada.

Available at your local bookstore or return this form to:

 CHARTER BOOKS
Book Mailing Service
P.O. Box 690, Rockville Centre, NY 11571

Please send me the titles checked above. I enclose _____ Include 75¢ for postage and handling if one book is ordered; 25¢ per book for two or more not to exceed $1.75. California, Illinois, New York and Tennessee residents please add sales tax.

NAME_____

ADDRESS_____

CITY_____STATE/ZIP_____

(allow six weeks for delivery.)   A8